The Littlest Warrior

Rebecca Bryan-Howell

"Do not let your hearts be troubled. Trust in God; trust also in me...I am going... to prepare a place for you. And if I go...I will come back and take you to be with me...I am the way and the truth and the life. No one comes to the Father except through me."
John 14:1-6

Jesus said, "Let the little children come to me, and do not hinder them, for the kingdom of God belongs to such as these...And he took the children in His arms...and blessed them."
Mark 10:14 & 16

The Littlest Warrior

© 2009 by Rebecca Bryan-Howell

PrismOfLife.com

Unless otherwise noted, all scripture quotations are taken from the HOLY BIBLE, NEW INTERNATIONAL VERSION®. Copyright © 1973, 1978, 1984 International Bible Society. Used by permission of Zondervan. All rights reserved.

The "NIV" and "New International Version" trademarks are registered in the United States Patent and Trademark Office by International Bible Society. Use of either trademark requires the permission of International Bible Society.

Scripture quotations marked "NKJV™" are taken from the New King James Version®. Copyright © 1982 by Thomas Nelson, Inc. Used by permission. All rights reserved.

Cover design by Calvin Bryant

ALL RIGHTS RESERVED

No part of this publication may be reproduced, stored in a retrieval system, or transmitted, in any form or by any means—electronic, mechanical, photocopying, recording, or otherwise—without prior written permission.

Printed in the United States of America

Dedicated to my wonderful daughter,
Angela Cheri´

Always my angel—
God's messenger to me in so many ways
—I cherish you.
Your enthusiasm for life is a beautiful gift;
Your determination in the face of difficulty,
a remarkable strength;
Your faith in God, a radiant light—on your pathway,
and upon others whose paths you cross.
Keep looking up.
Love Always,
Mom

To Pete, my favorite son-in-law:
You are God's man, and one of exceptional purpose.
May the great Trust He has bestowed upon you
direct your every endeavor.

To my grandsons: Tristyn, Bailey and Derek
God has ordained you for great things. Keep His
Truth in your heart, and His Ultimate Plan as your
compass. The battle is the Lord's.

To Delaney Isabelle:
You are The Rainbow, a priceless gift of Love.
Laughter and song will be yours. ♪

In Loving Memory of Bradey Josheb Markis

*With heartfelt appreciation,
    I would like to thank
        my loving husband, Jim,*

*who has provided the opportunity
    for me to pursue my writing;
        and who, with other family
    members and close friends,
        has encouraged me*

*from the first stroke of inspiration
    through the finished manuscript
        of this amazing, God-given story.*

Table of Contents

Guide to Character Names 7

Ode to Bradey 9

Author's Note 11

Chapter 1: Called Away 13

Chapter 2: The Grand Reception................... 23

Chapter 3: A Ride with the King 35

Chapter 4: Kids' Paradise 49

Chapter 5: Champion Ranch 63

Chapter 6: A Grandmother's Garden 77

Chapter 7: The Chronicles of Time.............. 99

Chapter 8: Bradey's Rainbow 117

Chapter 9: Commissioned............................ 133

Chapter 10: Training Camp 151

Chapter 11: Bradey's Battalion 175

Chapter 12: The Sound of the Trumpet.... 189

Guide to Character Names Meanings and Pronunciations

Anchorr .... Ang′kor
   From "anchor – to secure firmly"
Charu′ (Indian) "Beautiful" .... Shä roo′
Cordero Milagro Joaquin (Spanish) .... Wä keen′
   "Little lamb" "Miracle" "Raised by Yahweh"
Damien Xander (Greek) .... Dā′ mēən Zặn′der
   "To tame, subdue" "Defender of Men"
Ekundayo (African-Yoruba) .... Ēkūn day′ō
   "Sorrow becomes Joy"
Grant Finlay (Scottish) .... Fin′lee
   "Great" "Fair Warrior"
Gunnar Jens (Scandinavian) .... Gū′ner Jenz
   "Battle Warrior" "God is Gracious"
Hagan .... Hā′gən
   "Protector"
Iniko Ajani Diallo (African) .... In ē′kō Äjä′nē Dē äl′ō
   "born in troubled times" "he who wins the struggle" "bold"
Ivan Alexei (Russian) .... Ī′vən Alex′ē
   "God is Gracious" "Defender"
Jabari Faris Mansour .... Jəbär′ē Fär ēs′ Män sūr′
   "Fearless" "Knight" "One who Triumphs"
Jai (Sanskrit) "Victory" .... Jī
Jangi "Warrior" .... Joŋ gē′
Leo Dante (Italian/Latin) .... Lē′ō Dän′tay
   "Lion" "Everlasting"
Nevan Kane (Irish) .... Něv′ən Kāyn
   "Little Saint" "Battle"
Philyra (Greek) "Love of Music" .... Fəlēr′ə
Raj (India) "King" .... Razh
Reece Ryder (Australian) .... Rēs Rī′der
   "Running" "Knight; Mounted Warrior)
Sheng Li (Chinese) .... Shěŋ Lē
   "Victory" "Powerful"
Simcha (Hebrew) "Joy; festivity" .... Sïm′ kə
Stefan Kaiser (German) ....Stě′fən Kī′zer
   "Crown" "Leader"
Uzi Seth-Kenan Zacharee .... Ū′zē Seth-Kē′nən Ză′kərē
   "Power & Strength" "Appointed-to take possession"
        "God has remembered"
Yashobam (Hebrew) .... Yä′shōbäm
   "The troops will return"

Little Warrior

Little Warrior of our hopes,
We had thought to keep you longer;
Not to see you slip away
 Even before the close of day.

While so lovingly I gave you
All the strength my heart would hold,
God ordained a different role;
As the Captain of your soul.

Now I hold you—cherished moment—
Knowing, though I sorrow for you,
In your peaceful, infant rest,
God, your Maker, knows what's best.

He has shown me, by your presence,
On this day that He has given,
How he might fulfill my plea;
Had it been the best for me.

In His Providence Divine,
Though the world misunderstand,
You are spared from pain and strife;
He has weaned you from this life.

To His arms we now commend you,
Little one who held my heart.
Hope will always help me see
My son waiting there for me.

--April 27, 2007 by Rebecca Bryan-Howell—

A Note from the Author

Bradey was taken from our world as an infant, before he had the chance to experience life among us on this Earth. He will always be missed, although we know that he is in a better place.

We cannot laugh and play with him in the physical realm that confines our souls for yet awhile longer; but we can imagine his joy in the spiritual realm where he now resides; and where we will join him some day soon when Christ returns for His own.

So dry your tears of sadness, and come with me to a place where all goodness and pleasure abound; where dreams are reality and love and laughter flourish. Think of our little one in a land where sorrow and disappointment will never cloud his days; where evil will never stalk his tender soul.

Let your spirit be lifted to a new level of hope and anticipation. Free your mind from the human limits of fear and philosophy, and open your heart to imagine freely how wonderful Heaven must be! Come with me to another realm, where the possibilities are endless; a place of unparalleled beauty and profound peace; where God lives; and where our loved ones--who have gone ahead to join the ranks of the redeemed--wait to greet us at our journey's end; just inside the Pearly Gates.

Called Away

A tiny soul, safe and secure in a mother's womb, leaped suddenly in its minuscule, human shell. Perfectly formed, the little boy's body would be a beautiful place for the tiny soul to reside; and to live out its time on the planet Earth, as expected. This little soul, however, tugged persistently at the miniature human heart with every rhythmic beat, its fervent whispers echoing inside the uterine walls, "Come, Little Warrior! Come! The Master calls you; come quickly! Come now!"

The little heart hesitated, sensing the mother's love; hearing her soft voice beckoning him to come into her waiting arms; feeling her caressing hands move over the surface of his pre-birth home, getting as close as she could to the child she had carried these eight-plus months. The tiny, beating heart longed to stay and discover life among the voices he had become so accustomed to hearing around him day after day: the calm, measured voice that was brief but caring; the soft, slightly raspy and questioning voice that hovered more often with loving curiosity and small pats on the wall; the small, excitable voice that erupted regularly with giggles and enthusiasm, daily hugging the burgeoning orb and saying, "Is this my bwutho?" The little heart yearned to be cradled by the one whose voice soothed his little nerves and relaxed his tiny muscles again and again as he kicked against the walls of his confining bubble; and to see the face of the strong, low voice that always came the very closest at night—the one that made his habitat reverberate with every word, and seemed to be ever attended by a series of pats and rubs that jiggled and jostled the little person inside while at the same time providing a sense of great security.

THE LITTLEST WARRIOR

Surrounded by this environment of constant and varied emotions pulling from the outside, the little soul heard another voice from far away, faintly but firmly calling his name. And while the little human heart beat in rhythm with his mother's heartbeat in the womb-- the only place of safety and comfort he had ever known-- his tiny but eternal soul marched to a different drum, and began to pull away, tugging toward a place that, however mysterious, drew the little heart more and more until finally with a kick and a leap, the little soul broke free and went soaring upward in a vacuum of light and strength.

As the little soul tumbled about in this vibrant, moving radiance, strong hands encased it gently but firmly, so that perfect balance was restored; and the turbulence from the abrupt transition began to fall farther and farther behind. Instead of jostling and noise, confusion and apprehension, the little soul became steady and calm—with joyful anticipation—as it was lifted speedily away; and along with the balance came acute knowledge and understanding, which enabled the little soul to realize that he had left behind a family who waited to love him and a world that had waited to welcome him. This realization caused him to wonder; but before the first question could pop into being, he glided through a Golden Gate and slid to a stop on his heavenly little bottom, looking with great surprise into the face of a mighty, winged Being who towered above him.

A broad smile spread across the smooth, bronze face; the sea-green eyes twinkled merrily and two bushy, golden eyebrows rose expectantly as Heaven's newest arrival was lifted into the arms of his Guardian Angel.

"I am Anchorr (Ang′ kor)," he said.

Then a deep, rich chuckle rolled over his curved lips, and as he tilted his head back to let out a river of boisterous laughter, the little soul noticed a big dimple in Anchorr's strong, square chin. Then the Guardian gave him a comfy squeeze and said, "Bradey Josheb! Welcome to The Master's Heaven; He's been calling you!"

The cherub jostled himself in the arms of the gigantic angel now, and put one chubby little arm around his neck. Then looking intently into the sea-green eyes of the Guardian with his own of chocolate brown he asked with intense concern yet unblemished confidence,

"Anchorr, who will look after my mother?"

"A true warrior," Anchorr nodded with admiration, "whose first concern is not for himself, but for the welfare of those he is commissioned to protect. And you will have an active role in this protection from your place in Heaven, but come; I will show you how the Father has provided for her in your temporary absence. We must hurry; there is festivity afoot, and *you* are the guest of honor!"

Lifting the cherub, Anchorr began to run; but it seemed as if his feet never touched the ground. He held Bradey securely in his powerful arms as the distant hills that they had seen from the Golden Gate loomed ever closer until suddenly appearing in front of them as towering mountains. Anchorr raised one arm skyward, straight as an arrow; and with a surge of power that made Bradey tingle from heavenly head to toe, they were instantly at the top of the mountain range where a beautiful rainbow arched across the sky. Of course, these things were all new to Bradey Josheb because he had not learned about mountains, or running, or rainbows on Earth; and he was fascinated! Questions tumbled from his cherry-cherub lips as fast as Anchorr could answer them, and when he was finally so spellbound by the glittering colors of the rainbow that he could no longer speak, Anchorr stretched forth one giant hand into Heaven's blue and looked at Bradey with a knowing grin saying,

"Ready?"

"Yup," the cherub whispered, holding his breath; and a very yellow curl popped onto his shiny forehead as he peered ahead with the greatest intrigue.

As Anchorr snapped his fingers—producing an electric POP! that echoed across the sound waves, the bright blue sky rolled up to reveal a deep, midnight blue dotted with billions of twinkling stars.

Bradey caught his breath, "Ahhh! What are those?"

"They are The Master's night lights; but we will learn of those later. Look deeper now; through the stars to that rosy glow very far away…" and as Bradey focused on the dim light on the other side of the stars, the scene zoomed closer until it appeared before him like a theater stage; and the questions began again.

It was a beautiful place with flowers and trees and rolling grassy knolls. A small group of somber people stood around a canopy, where others who were all dressed up sat in pretty chairs looking forward to a small, white box with blue and white flowers on its top. Tears were streaming down their faces and a man in front was talking about Heaven. Of course, Anchorr had to explain all of this to Bradey, because he had never learned about trees and flowers, or people, or dressing up, or earthly tears. Anchorr patiently waited as the little cherub scanned the scenes below, answering every question that Bradey posed. He pointed out Bradey's grandpas and grandmas, aunts and uncles and cousins, explaining each human term to the curious child. As he explained that the tiny baby inside the white box was Bradey's earthly body before he left for Heaven, the cherub glanced at his own hands and feet with amazement, and reached his chubby fingers up to squeeze his blonde, curly hair—and he was instantly pleased at how *much* he had grown on his trip from Earth!

Suddenly Bradey spotted three fine-looking young boys in very tidy, matching clothes and pointed them out, saying, "Do I know them?"

"Yes, you do!" Anchorr, chuckled. "The tall one with big, brown eyes is the *calm and measured* voice; the one you did not hear so often, but always waited to hear again; The next one with crinkled eyebrows and sea-green eyes—like mine—is the voice *full of questions and curiosity* that talked to you often through the wall of your mother's womb; and that little one, with the bright blue eyes who holds your grandmother's hand is the small, excited voice that giggled around you every day while he awaited your birth—these are your brothers."

Bradey gazed at each of them with awe, and with a slight smile said softly, "I love them; I love my brothers."

Then with a sudden crinkle in his brow, very much like his middle brother with the sea-green eyes, he asked,

"But what about the other voice, the *strong, low voice that was closest to me at night*?"

Anchorr smiled broadly, "Your Dad...see him, right there in front?" and as Anchorr pointed through the portal, Bradey grinned from ear to ear, reaching forward as if to caress the voice and the touch that he remembered so well, and he wondered aloud.

"Will my dad carry me on his strong shoulders like you do, Anchorr?"

But before his Guardian could answer, Bradey heard another familiar sound, like music to his ears; frail and sweet, whispering his name. And as his brown eyes became large with recognition and a tingle went down his little spine, he gasped excitedly.

"I *know* that voice!" and searching the crowd intently, he found her on the first row beside his dad and pointed with pride, "My mother, Anchorr. Isn't she beautiful? That's my mom."

Then, without warning, his little chin quivered and a rush of tears like tiny diamonds flooded his angelic eyes and spilled over onto his rosy cherub cheeks. He swiped a dimpled hand over his eyes, looked questioningly up at Anchorr and quizzed him.

"...but, if tears are *earthly*, then what are these?"

With a soft pat on the little back and a gentle brush of his giant thumb across the child's cheek, the Guardian said softly.

"These beautiful diamond tears are something that my kind does not fully understand. You must ask The

Master. But I have heard that the inhabitants of Heaven can feel the sorrow of their earthly loved ones, and that they cry tears of compassion for them. There is no Sorrow here, but there is Love; and it is told in the camps of the Guardians that Compassion is the flower of a loving heart."

Bradey blinked and watched his tears fall the great distance from where he sat in Anchorr's arms to the grassy hillside below his feet. With fascination and delight, he noticed that as each teardrop hit the ground a beautiful flower sprang up on the spot! He climbed down from his Guardian's strong embrace and wandered on the hillside, feeling the cool grass on his rosy feet—a wonderful sensation that, of course, was all new to him. He began to pick the flowers that grew from his tears, one by one, looking through the portal as he gathered them, into his sweet mother's tear-stained face. He wanted to wrap his chunky little arms around her neck and hug her tight and tell her that he was alright, and that he was picking her a bouquet that she would love; but suddenly the gleaming hues of the rainbow above caught his eye again and the flowers he had picked drooped slightly at his side.

Gazing once more through the portal, he said softly, "I don't really want to send her flowers, Anchorr;" then, running back to his Guardian and looking him full in the face with great satisfaction, he smiled pleasantly and announced as Anchorr lifted him to his great shoulders, "I want to send her a *rainbow*!"

And with his rolling laughter filling the hillside, Anchorr boomed, "And so you shall, my Little Warrior; and so you shall!"

They both turned then to look through the portal as Anchorr continued, "King Jesus has already heard your request and He has the perfect rainbow in mind. When the time is right, He will send it to Earth with His blessing."

Bradey was pleased to no end that his mother would get a rainbow from Heaven sometime soon; but he wondered aloud, "I hope I don't miss it; I hope it makes her very, very happy, Anchorr."

"She will be very happy indeed, Bradey Josheb; and I am very sure that The Master will have you ushered to the portal with haste to witness the arrival of the special gift that you requested of Him."

Bradey took a deep breath and then sighed with satisfaction, "That's good!"

Then, as if the happy ending of a rainbow suddenly justified his small bunch of flowers, he tossed his little bouquet gently toward the portal and it was instantly whisked into the other world in perfect form. Bradey watched it go and saw that his mom, at the same time, was touching the casket and placing a long-stemmed orange rose beside it with the greatest care. As she looked up with tears, folding her hands against her bosom, she drew in a sudden breath as Bradey's bouquet slipped perfectly into her clasped hands.

"She's not looking at my flowers," Bradey questioned. "Can she see them?"

"No," Anchorr answered with low tones that sounded sad and reverent at the same time. "But she can feel them in her heart. And look! She's sending something back to you."

Bradey turned to the scene below once again to see his beautiful, sorrowing mother blow a kiss heavenward, which lit upon Bradey's cherubic forehead as softly as a falling snowflake. Then in the twinkling of an eye, while the orange rose appeared to remain beside the white casket on earth, the heavenly version came soaring through the portal and slipped neatly into Bradey's dimpled fist; and in the place of every thorn along the stem there grew instead a dew-shaped diamond—his mother's tears.

As the Guardian gave the signal to close the portal, Bradey peered lovingly once more at the scene below, memorizing each face, especially his brothers'; and as he fingered the silky white ribbon on his orange rose he gazed intently at his mother one more time and spoke instinctively.

"But, Anchorr, where *is* The Master? My mother needs Him right now!"

"We will go to Him, Bradey Josheb. But He has heard your request and dispatched His messengers already. Look below."

As the portal began to recede and the blue skies of Heaven to return, Bradey saw a band of angels around his mother on Earth. They touched her on all sides, resting her head on their chest, loving her, holding her close, touching her aching heart, whispering hope into her ear, covering her with peace, and surrounding her with safety.

It was a beautiful sight to behold, and as Anchorr turned to go, Bradey sighed with satisfaction as only a little boy who feels very significant can do and stated matter-of-factly.

"Well, I guess that will do for now. Can you tell me more about my brothers?"

Anchorr, for an instant, wondered if he felt a twinge of what the humans call 'regret'. He had only been assigned to this tiny liege for a very short time; and now that Bradey was in Heaven, his assignment would soon be over. But as he strode across the hillsides toward the Golden Gate, he wondered how anything could be better than tending Bradey Josheb Markis and he was pleased – as pleased as an angel can possibly be—that they could spend a little more time together before he was re-assigned to Earth.

"Well," he began with a broad grin; "your eldest brother loves big machines; he wants to be a pilot..." and he continued as best he could, in between myriads of questions, to describe the brothers to Bradey. He remembered that the middle brother adored God's animal kingdom; and then tried to get a word in about the smallest brother wanting to win everything, and that it was indicative of his bold, victorious nature. But finally, he decided that this task would be better served by The Master himself; so he concluded, as he lifted Bradey to a wall of gemstones.

"You will have to take up the rest of your questions with The Master, my little friend. He made your brothers, so he can explain *everything*. But right now, there is a celebration ready to begin, and some very special people are waiting to see you."

-2-
The Grand Reception

Bradey heard something in the distance and began to stretch and strain his eyes and ears toward the sound. It was music and singing, both of which Anchorr had to explain. He moved swiftly along a beautiful pathway lined with large, swaying trees with leaves of all colors. Blue, red, and yellow birds launched their musical songs from branch to branch while butterflies with green and purple paisley wings fluttered overhead. Bradey saw so many things that he wanted to stop and investigate, but he knew that his Guardian was on a mission and he wisely decided not to ask any more questions. Soon the landscape opened into something like a huge park, with flowers and benches, fountains and gardens in every direction. Directly in the center was a large structure of ivory and gold, with tall, majestic pillars at the entry way and a spacious courtyard in front where people meandered around talking and laughing together. Bradey noticed right away that there were lots of little ones like him.

Suddenly the bright, clear sound of a horn pierced through the noise of happy chatter and brought all the party guests to attention; and in the next instant all eyes were on Anchorr and Bradey as they entered the courtyard through a silver-lattice gate. Bradey felt a bit awkward with everyone staring at him, even though they were all smiling as he and Anchorr made their way through the crowd; and they were saying nice things like, "Look at that curly hair!" and "What a beautiful child he is!"

The comment he heard most often, however, was "Ah, look! The Mother's Kiss!"

This exclamation left Bradey quite confused, for he did not know that, in Heaven, the last kiss of a Mother where her lips rested as she whispered her final 'goodbye' shines on in Eternity like a dainty silver snowflake upon her child's rosy face.

Then Anchorr stepped up onto a platform in front of the assembly and lifted Bradey from his shoulders to a nearby column where everyone could see him.

"Family and friends," Anchorr addressed them in his low, booming voice, "we have gathered here together to celebrate the arrival of Bradey Josheb Markis, the Littlest Warrior!"

Joyous shouts went up all around, as people tossed wreaths into the air and waved colorful flags above their heads. Bradey was filled with excitement as his head turned this way and that. He was awestruck that all these people had come to welcome him and was scanning their faces with great curiosity, wondering who they all were, when a particularly noticeable chant at the back of the crowd caught his attention. It was coming from a group of very muscular fellows with shiny golden shields held high.

"One Cause! One Conqueror! One King!"

As they shouted in unison, Bradey felt a shiver go down his angelic spine and his eyes grew wide with wonder as he whispered to Anchorr.

"Do they know me?"

THE GRAND RECEPTION

Anchorr chuckled and said, "They know *about* you and have been waiting to meet The Master's Littlest Warrior. You will find out more about them very soon; here comes their Captain now."

Bradey watched with amazement as a strong, stocky man made his way through the crowd. He was dressed in battle gear and his armored shin-guards clinked and rattled with every step he took. He had a bushy, black beard trimmed short around his face and his dark eyes were stern but kind as he strode up to the pillar where Bradey stood.

Turning first to Anchorr, he grasped his massive arm firmly and said with the greatest respect, "Anchorr, Guardian of Warriors; greetings, my friend!"

Then he put out his hand and spoke with a big smile and a raspy voice.

"Welcome home, Bradey Josheb. I am Yashobam."

Bradey knew about handshakes because Anchorr had lost no time in teaching him this kingdom greeting, the "heavenly man-shake". So with confidence and pride, he reached out past the warrior's hand to grasp his thick, brawny forearm as firmly as his chubby palm could manage, answering stoutly.

"Yes, sir!" (Which Anchorr had also taught him.)

"That's my little man!" Yashobam bellowed with a jolly guffaw that revealed a row of large, very white teeth below a dark mustache.

"You are my namesake, you know!"

THE LITTLEST WARRIOR

Bradey grinned as he memorized Yashobam's face, noting that he had a very obvious split between his two front teeth; and then feeling the back of his own little teeth with his tongue to see if he had one, too. Yashobam was gesturing toward the rest of his men, who responded with raised swords, gleaming in the Light of the Lamb.

"The men want to meet you. We will talk again, after the celebration," he said with a shoulder squeeze and a tousling of Bradey's yellow locks.

As Yashobam strode away, Bradey quizzed Anchorr, "What is a *namesake*?"

Anchorr's sea-green eyes widened slightly as he looked after Yashobam with evident admiration and answered.

"A namesake is one who is given another's name. You were named after Yashobam because he was a mighty warrior in the time of the prophets of old. He served under a great man—a man after God's own heart, who became one of the greatest kings to ever rule The Chosen. Yashobam risked his life again and again for The Ultimate Plan and he defeated 300 enemies in one encounter with his own spear."

"Did you *see* it, Anchorr? Were you there?" Bradey asked with eyes full of awe.

"Yes...I was there...right by his side."

He spoke slowly, as if he was remembering it all over again; and after a long pause, Anchorr perched a large hand on the back of Bradey's shoulders and added an after-thought.

THE GRAND RECEPTION

"He is your mentor and he will teach you all the strategies of war; you will learn the ways of the Heavenly Warriors; you will walk in Yashobam's footsteps."

Bradey looked down suddenly at his own small, chubby feet and wriggled his pink toes.

"I sure hope I can keep up," he chirped merrily, wondering how he would look in Yashobam's big boots.

Anchorr lifted Bradey to his shoulder again and strode through the massive entry into Celebration Hall. He walked to a large table at the front of the great room. There were several people seated at the table and there was one empty seat in the middle that was a high-backed chair with gold, ornamental scrolling; Bradey wondered if it was for him. The people all rose from their seats when they saw Anchorr and Bradey, and one man with dark hair and a glad smile came forward and spoke to them.

"So this is the guest of honor! Come over here, Bradey, and give your grandpa a squeeze!"

Bradey felt very loved by this man, but was a little confused, since Anchorr had already pointed out his two grandpas through the portal at the earthly Memorial Service.

"I thought my grampas were still on earth," he said, looking into the face of this man who had sort of a round nose and a big crease around each side of his mouth when he smiled.

THE LITTLEST WARRIOR

"They are," the man answered. "But I'm your *great*-grandpa!" And he nipped the cherub's little nose between his knuckles.

"Yessiree, Bradey-boy! Hee-heee!" said another voice close by.

Bradey peeked over the edge of Great-grandpa's shoulder to see another grinning man with gray hair and very blue eyes who winked and said, "And I'm even *greater* than him, don't ya know!"

The first great-grandpa turned to face the other one with a chuckle and explained.

"This is my dad, and your Great-great-grandpa, Doc. He was kinda old on Earth, but up here he's good as new!" after which quip both grandfathers laughed heartily once again.

"You betcha, Bradey-boy!" Greater-grandpa Doc responded with a wave of his hand and a nod of his head. "Now, Gail, give that fine boy some food!"

Bradey looked for the first time at the feast before them. Every table was loaded with the most delicious fare imaginable, and everyone wanted to introduce Bradey to their favorite delights. He tasted food for the first time and learned the savory diversity between sweet and tart; soft and crunchy; juicy and dry; pungent and mild. He watched with great interest as people ate and drank and laughed and talked all around him in the great hall, while skilled dancers and musicians performed artistically on center stage.

Bradey got hugged and kissed and squeezed and teased by everybody who came by his table, and he was amazed at how large his Heavenly family was! The people at the head table with him turned out to be a mixture of grandpas, grandmas, aunts, uncles, and cousins. Each one presented him a special gift, and Anchorr produced a shiny pouch into which Bradey placed his treasures to look at again later. He had a rope woven of gold, silver, and copper cords; a miniature spade of pure nickel with a copper handle, and many other items of intrigue. His favorite, however, was a bright white sailboat with blue lettering that said, *From Robert with Love* on the bow.

He was fascinated to see that the pouch stayed small enough to fit neatly and comfortably on his belt, even though he stuffed all his gifts inside. It didn't bulge or gape open; in fact, it still looked flat as if it was empty. Bradey looked quizzically at Anchorr who chuckled merrily.

"It's called a *Miracle Pocket* because it stays the same size no matter what you put inside; but when you open it to take something out, you will find all your treasures safe and sound."

So the cherub's heavenly schedule was already filling up with exciting places to go and more people to see. Bradey laughed and chattered and thoroughly enjoyed being the life of the party. He met members of his family who were musicians, singers, gardeners, orators, artists, builders, preachers and warriors; and he discovered that they were all great story-tellers who could keep him totally enraptured with their tales of adventure. Anchorr also introduced Bradey to many other Guardians like himself, who were between assignments; and of course, he met the rest of Yashobam's men and gave each of them the heavenly man-shake.

Finally, there was a commotion at the back of Celebration Hall by the door; and all the guests began to exclaim with "oooo's" and "aaaah's" about something that Bradey Josheb was too short to see!

"What is it, Anchorr?" he stuttered with excitement. But Anchorr had already started toward the door to offer his assistance. So Greater-grandpa Doc lifted Bradey to a table top where he could see above people's heads. Two big animals were coming into the hall carrying a platform between them. On the platform was a huge delicacy that was at least three feet tall and four feet wide; and Grandpa Doc exclaimed.

"Well, Bradey-boy; look'ee here! A couple o' big cats is a-bringin' us dessert! Look at them tigers a-carrying that birthday cake! If that don't beat all!" Of course, Bradey had never seen a birthday cake *or* a tiger, so all the relatives chimed in to explain them to him, but it was Great-grandpa Gail who solved the mystery.

"Bradey, when you looked through the portal, did Anchorr show you the little, short grandma with the curly, brown hair?"

Bradey nodded, "Uh-huh."

"Well," Great-grandpa continued, "she's your grandma *now*; but before she grew up and got old, she was my little girl. We've all been having a great time with your welcome celebration, but today is her birthday, too! So, wha'd'ya say we let her in on the party and sing her the birthday song?"

After a quick explanation from one of the great-grandmothers about earthly birthdays with cake and song, Bradey nodded an enthusiastic, "Yes, let's!"

THE GRAND RECEPTION

All at once, the great hall was filled with cheerful music as Great-grandpa began to lead out in his fine melodic voice, "A Happy Birthday to you, A Happy Birthday to you. May you feel Jesus near every day of the year…" after which, Bradey erupted with many more questions; one of which was, "But can she hear us way up here?"

"Not with her ears," said Great-grandpa Gail, cocking his head to one side, as he lifted Bradey from the table top and plopped him onto his knee. "Just with her heart; and every year on her birthday, she will remember you and hear it again."

Bradey didn't quite get it, but he was satisfied for now; especially since it was time to taste the cake. For, as the guest of honor, he was offered the first piece. Bradey discovered, between mouthfuls of fluffy angel food with a fruit called 'strawberry', that the tigers were named Ebony and Alabaster, and that they stood at the gates of a special garden that he would visit sometime soon.

Then, a girl-cousin in a silky blue gown beaded with silver and pearls made her way to center stage as harps and flutes began to play. She was tall and slender and her light auburn hair flowed like silk in the breeze as she walked gracefully forward. Her large hazel eyes twinkled brightly when she turned around, and she smiled sweetly at Bradey as if to welcome him one more time.

He waved a dimpled hand in response and asked, "Who is that again?" to which several grandparents began to contribute various answers all at once.

THE LITTLEST WARRIOR

Her name was Sarah, and she had been called to Heaven just before she was born, just like him. Bradey was so enraptured by the harps that played and the song she sang, that he did not notice the reverent silence that soon fell over the crowded hall; or the heads that bowed in honor as she sang.

"All praise to Thee, Oh King of Kings; The Lord of Lords to whom the whole earth sings; we lift you high; and give you glory! We bow the knee, to worship Thee!"

At that moment, as the last sweet note fell silent on Sarah's lips, a bright light filled the room and Bradey looked wide-eyed toward the entrance, only to squint and blink and cover his curious eyes with two chubby hands. Anchorr had spoken to Bradey of this encounter when they had first arrived. He had explained that Heaven's King, who was both Lion and Lamb, would be coming soon to show Bradey around the place. Anchorr had explained that this King was The Master of the Universe to whom all creation sang; and that it was His voice that had called The Little Warrior up from the earth that day.

Now, peeking through his fingers, Bradey saw a magnificent Being enter the hall, and heard a voice like the roll of thunder call his name; a voice that had called him once before; a voice like no other. And though his little plump lip trembled as his big brown eyes looked upward into the Eyes of Fire before him, the Presence of the King enveloped the Littlest Warrior in the soft, peaceful Light of the Lamb, and a Love like he could never have imagined swept over his tiny frame as the great hand of The Master reached out to take his rosy, dimpled one.

THE GRAND RECEPTION

"Welcome to my Heaven, Bradey Josheb! Come, child, and walk with Me."

As The Master's hand pressed gently, covering Bradey's head, a great surge of warmth and strength went through his little body and sent a shiver of excitement down his angelic spine. At that moment he felt so big that he had no doubt he could most certainly follow in Yashobam's footsteps—*and* keep up—and learn everything his mentor taught him. Bradey did not know this yet, but what he felt just then was *confidence*; the kind The Master always uses to wrap up all His gift packages when he presents them to His stewards. The Master felt the power surge go from His own mighty Being into His Littlest Warrior, and He smiled when Bradey shivered from cherubic head to toe; for He knew exactly what the little one was feeling and how very excited he would be later on to discover what this mysterious exhilaration was all about.

The silence that had come over Celebration Hall at the entrance of the King was like a great, soft cloud that hovered in the atmosphere just above the people's heads; and Bradey supposed that it had gently pressed them all to their knees, because only now did he notice that everyone was bowing in the presence of the King of Heaven. Suddenly Bradey felt a bit awkward and bowed his own head quickly; but before he could close his eyes he felt himself being lifted higher and higher until he found himself cradled in the arm of The Master as He strode toward the open door. The light that surrounded Him was soft and comforting to Bradey, yet so bright that he could not see the people in the hall. It was as if he and the King were gliding through a glowing channel.

As they stepped out into the courtyard, all of Heaven erupted into sounds of exaltation to the Lord of All. Behind them, the people who were gathered in the grand hall erupted into praise and applause to the King; and outside the birds in the trees broke into cheerful song with a scale of notes that made Bradey's ears tingle. The air was full of music—from all kinds of instruments that Bradey had yet to learn about; and choirs of angels sang praises to the Most High in the distance, while their sweet voices wafted closer at sporadic intervals—as if someone kept turning up the music.

"Jesus is Lord!" "Hail to the King of Heaven!" "All praise to the Son of God!" "Honor and glory to the Lamb!" lauding The Master as He walked through His Heaven.

Bradey suddenly realized that he was in the arms of the Greatest One of All; and he felt very happy, very safe and very much loved in the ultra-powerful embrace of King Jesus. His thrills were just beginning, however; for little did he know the incredible adventures that awaited him in this matchless wonderland. In fact, one of these great adventures awaited him now. It stood pert and guarded at the edge of the crowd, eyeing with energetic curiosity this tiny new object of The Master's tender delight.

A Ride with the King

As The King of Heaven neared the edge of the courtyard amidst the praise of his subjects and all the creatures of Heaven, Bradey caught sight of something outside the gate that took his breath away. There was a magnificent white horse with striking eyes of the deepest blue, prancing and pawing the ground. His main of soft, wispy curls hung half way to the ground and his tail touched the grass behind him. Both were woven with tiny cords of purple and gold that made them glitter as he tossed his head and swished his tail. The crimson red velvet coverlet on his broad back had golden trim and golden tassels, and it's deep, rich color made the beautiful animal's bright, white coat gleam like glass. Bradey was totally enraptured by this creature and did not even notice that The Master had stopped in front of it until The Master spoke.

"Bradey Josheb, how would you like to ride my horse?" Then, without hesitation, the King lifted the cherub onto its back and said, "Be still, Champion."

The mighty creature stamped his great hooves gently and then stood perfectly still before the King.

"Well, what do you think, Bradey?" The Master smiled.

"I *love* him, King Jesus!" Bradey squealed with such enthusiasm that Champion danced in a half circle with his back feet and tried to look back at the tiny little person sitting on his back.

Bradey was not the slightest bit frightened and he instinctively leaned forward and hugged the great white neck. The Master's laughter rolled across the landscape, even farther than Anchorr's, as he patted Bradey on the back and placed the reins in one little hand, while Bradey clung precariously to his mother's rose with the other. The reins were woven of gold, silver and bronze strands that felt soft against Bradey's little palm. As he studied them, he realized that they matched the coil of rope that The Grandfathers had given him at the reception; but he did not have enough hands to open his Miracle Pocket and look, so he decided he would check it out after the ride with The Master.

"Champion will follow me;" The Master said. "You don't need to guide him, but I want you to get the feel of the reins in your hand, so you must sheath your Mother's Rose for this ride. Very soon you will have a steed of your own and you must learn how to handle him."

"I get my very own *hoss*?" Bradey was weak with astonishment, slowly stroking Champion's mane with his chubby hand.

The Master laughed again at the Littlest Warrior's pronunciation of the word and said, "Yes, my Little Warrior, your very own *hoss*; and I am very pleased to see that you are taking so naturally to the art of the Heavenly Riders!" For The King had noticed that Bradey had instinctively woven the reins into the fingers of his right hand just like the pros.

At the same time, Bradey noticed a small, slender sheath that hung from his belt next to his miracle pouch. He carefully slid the tear-studded stem of his orange rose into the sheath, and took great delight in the fact that it fit perfectly, and would keep his cherished blossom safely at his side whenever his hands were too busy to hold it.

The King began to walk down the Golden Road and Bradey sat high on Champion's back taking in all the sights and sounds. He was a bit shy about asking questions in the presence of the King, but once in awhile he blurted one out before he could think to hold it in. Most of the time, he was so enraptured by the fantastic ride that he thought of nothing else; so he was very surprised when Champion stopped and turned around, prancing on all fours like only the real champions do.

They had followed the Golden Road up to the top of a high, grassy hill where the yellow and violet flowers began to sway from side to side. Bradey had noticed during his ride, that wherever The King passed by, all the trees, flowers and grasses in Heaven would gently sway in His presence as if they were waving their greetings to their king. Bradey looked below from their place on the hill and saw beautiful things in every direction without end. He was fascinated as The Master pointed out the River of Life, the Sea of Glass, and various gardens, structures and points of interest all over Heaven. Then he pointed far away to a side of Heaven where a golden glow hid everything from view like a bright, billowing cloud.

"There is My Father's House," The Master said with great reverence in His deep, pure voice. "His throne is in the midst of that golden glow, surrounded by angels and cherubim who worship Him continually. That's where most of the music of Heaven comes from. God's Throne is the center of the Heavenly Realm; so all that you see from this hilltop is only a small part of Heaven. There is this much more to see from all sides of the

Father's House. You will have many places to explore."

Then King Jesus took Bradey into His arms again and told Champion to go nibble some sweet grass for awhile. King Jesus pointed out a few more things that he wanted Bradey to see from the hilltop: The Great Hall of Music; The Champion Ranch where all the heavenly horses lived and were trained for The Master's service; a place called Kids' Paradise; and Camp Conquest where Yashobam trained all the warriors, just to name a few.

Bradey was so excited that he could not possibly hold in all the questions. Some of the most explosive ones that escaped his quivering ruby lips were like: "Is the Great Hall of Music where my Sarah learned to sing?" "Does my hoss live at Champion Ranch?" "When will I see Yashobam's training camp?" and etcetera. The King of Heaven took delight in every word from the cherub's mouth and answered every question to his boyish satisfaction.

Then He sat down on the flowing grass and said, "Now I want you to lean back on my chest while I tell you some very important things about why I brought you here."

Bradey thought the lap of The Master must be the most comfortable place in Heaven. He was completely peaceful and happy as he listened to the words of the great king. King Jesus explained how much He loved all of his children, and that He had special things for all of them to do—some on Earth and some in Heaven. He told how everything that happens is a part of God's plan for mankind, and how some day all of His own would live close to Him in an everlasting Kingdom. He explained to Bradey about Satan, God's great enemy who roamed the Earth and ruled its atmosphere, and how crafty he was in his purpose to destroy the hope of God's people and to distract them from His Great Plan of the Ages.

As Bradey was listening, his tiny but brilliant mind understood every word and he began to lovingly stroke The Master's robe and hair and hands. Suddenly he felt something crinkly and rough in The Master's hand and he opened the great strong fingers to get a closer look. There in the center of that magnificent palm was a very ugly mark that looked like it did not even belong in Heaven, let alone on the hand of The King.

Bradey touched the scar gently and looked up into the face of his King, "What is this, King Jesus? Why is this on your hand?"

At this, The Master opened the other hand to reveal an identical scar in the center of it as well.

"These are my Scars of Love, Bradey. I have them on my feet, too. I keep them to remind the whole world that I came to rescue them from the enemy and to give them a way into Heaven."

Then something remarkable happened as Jesus spoke softly about his scars: this little cherub who had left the Earth before he ever had a chance to hear the Redemption Story suddenly knew it all. His little heart began to beat to the "ba-rumpa-bum-pum" of the little drummer boy as Bradey felt in his little spirit the miraculous truth of the Christmas story when Jesus came to Earth as a babe. Tears flowed down his little cheeks and he hid his face in the folds of Jesus' robe as he heard and understood the story of that cruel crucifixion of Christ, God's only son, and Jesus held him tightly as he wept. Then the words of Jesus fell upon Bradey's little being with quiet strength as He told the Resurrection Story of how He rose from the grave to conquer Death and Hell. At that moment, a thrill of exhilaration coursed through Bradey's little body and his spirit leaped within him at the realization that his King was the Champion of All Time, alive forevermore to reign over Heaven and Earth.

"You won!" he shouted like only little boys can do; and with a deep surge of relief and childish joy, Bradey hugged his master as tightly as he could and said, "I love you, King Jesus; You are my Hero." That moment birthed a bonding between the King of Heaven and His Littlest Warrior that went deeper than any human words could ever describe; and they just sat there together for awhile, loving every minute.

Then Jesus spoke again, standing Bradey up in front of him so He could look into his face.

"Bradey, your job is here in Heaven. You will do two very important things for me. First, you will watch your family and loved ones on Earth and you will tell me things about them; you are my messenger. Second, you will learn from Yashobam the ways of a warrior and we must begin soon; for you have much to learn and do. I have two more important things to show you before we descend to the city again; and then I will take you to the Father's House."

Without warning, King Jesus scooped up Bradey and leaped to Champion's back. Champion whinnied and pawed the ground and reared up in the air. Then with a powerful leap, the magnificent charger bounded over the edge of the hillside into a steep ravine of blue light.

A RIDE WITH THE KING

They were flying! Bradey's chubby fingers scrambled to grab a chunk of mane to hold onto, even though the strong arm of The Master held him securely; for the scenes below rolled by at a speed that would have caused any human boy to become very dizzy! Bradey sat like a proud warrior on his steed and soaked in the pure power of the ride as the Wind of Heaven rushed by his ears with a musical whir and ruffled his golden curls with every gust.

Then they landed on a mountain top; and though Champion's hooves came to a stop ever so gently, the ground beneath them rumbled as if it could hardly bear the power resonating from Heaven's King and his magnificent steed. The Heavenly Realm was far below, resembling a tiny toy city, and Champion seemed to be standing between two realms, as Bradey saw again the dark expanse full of stars that Anchorr had shown him once before. Suddenly, the darkness rolled back to reveal a scene on Earth, and through the portal Bradey saw his family again; his mom and dad and brothers. They were in a house eating supper together, and talking and laughing. Bradey wanted to touch them and Jesus felt his longing.

"You will see them soon, Bradey Josheb; you will welcome each of them to my Heaven. But until then you will see them from afar whenever you come to this portal on Mount Witness. While you are learning your new role, you will not come here alone; but with Anchorr or Yashobam. After every visit, you will call for me and I will answer you, just as you did the first day when you were concerned for your Mother. See her now? See the peace on her face. I am with her on Earth as surely as I am here with you in Heaven."

THE LITTLEST WARRIOR

Bradey felt very secure in The Master's arms, and somehow he knew that his mother was feeling the same thing. Reaching down to his sash he gently fingered his orange rose, just to make sure it was still there after his amazing flight through the skies of Heaven. Then remembering his Mother's Kiss Bradey gently touched his forehead under a wind-blown curl; and bringing both dimpled hands to his cherry lips he blew a kiss to the Earth. The King reached His great hand toward Bradey's family and blessed them through the portal as it began to close. He spoke softly at first and then louder and louder until Mount Witness trembled again beneath His feet. The heavens were echoing so deeply with The Master's great voice that Bradey thought surely his family *must* hear it. Then there was a small flash of light on Earth that sent Bradey's brothers running to the windows of their house to look outside.

"Awesome!" they all said as they peered through the glass; and Bradey's dad reached across the table to squeeze Mother's hand, smiling at her.

"Did they hear you, King Jesus?" Bradey asked with great curiosity as the portal disappeared.

"Yes," Jesus smiled; "but they thought it was thunder."

Bradey's eyes were still wide with wonder as Champion leaped into the air once again and glided through the heavens to another lofty peak. This mountain was not surrounded by a starry sky. Instead, a whispering wind blew continually and bolts of lightening broke the midnight blue expanse over and over again, followed by peals of thunder that rumbled and rolled all around them through a glimmering crystal mist.

A RIDE WITH THE KING

"Awesome!" Bradey exclaimed, deciding that the new word he had just learned from The Brothers was the only one that would work at a time like this. He figured if they said *Awesome!* about thunder, they would <u>surely</u> say it about all this! King Jesus had to explain "storms" to Bradey before he could open this portal to show him the next scene; because they were standing on Mount Imminent this time. Bradey was soon to learn of the great storms that would come upon the Earth, the great warrior that he was to become, and the Great Battle in which he would someday fight.

He held his baby breath as the portal began to open before him. There was a black, stormy sky and lots of dust, which Anchorr had told him about once before. Bradey heard shouts and much noise and the clanking of steel on steel coming from the scene before him; and as he strained his eyes to make out the forms in the dust cloud he thought he saw some strong men who looked very much like Yashobam's warriors for they were dressed in battle gear. They were all mounted on magnificent war horses. One of the youths was tall and strong with dark hair and intense dark eyes, searching the landscape; one was stocky and talkative, turning this way and that, fidgeting on his blue and silver coverlet; one was big and broad, looking strong enough to toss a horse. He had a giant silver shield and he was watching everything like a guardian; and the last, who talked and pointed as if he were showing the others what to do, was stern and muscular with bronze skin. He took off his red and gold helmet and shook his head of wavy golden hair.

"He has hair like mine!" Bradey pointed.

"That's because he *is you* all grown up, Bradey Josheb," the King answered, "and these elite warriors are part of your troops who will work side by side with you in the Great Battle at the End of Time."

Bradey trembled with anticipation, imagining what it must be like to be a grown up warrior fighting for the King of Kings as he studied the scene before him with wide eyes. Then he spoke with recollection.

"But haven't I seen them somewhere before?" Bradey questioned. "Do I know them?"

"Yes," the King answered softly, as a father who is pleased and proud. "They are your brothers."

Bradey was awestruck to see the Band of Brothers and even here in Heaven his little being was all aglow with a curious excitement made up of cold and heat, tingles and tears that sent shivers up and down his heavenly spine. He couldn't decide whether to shout or hide his face in the folds of the Master's robe.

"Awesome!" Bradey breathed as he took in the scene, putting his new word to good use. His little hands quivered against Champion's mane and his fingers took hold with a grip that made the great white steed prance and snort. King Jesus watched the whole scene with pride and joy, smiling as he saw the Heart of a Warrior shining through this tiny new recruit. But Bradey's next question brought that rolling laughter once again:

"King Jesus, how long does it take to get *all grown up?*"

"You will be *all grown up* whenever I decide you are ready, Bradey Josheb!" and the Master laughed again heartily as he turned Champion toward the valley below and shouted.

"Onward, to the Father's House!"

As they flew through the air, the atmosphere became light and balmy once again. The closer they came to the Center of Heaven the brighter the light shone; and instead of the brisk, cool air of the mountain peaks a warm, sweetly-scented breeze caressed their faces and the Choirs of Angels were louder than before. Champion's feet touched down at the base of the mountain where a thunderous roar filled the air. Bradey looked back to see a huge waterfall coursing down rocky cliffs at the foot of the mountain they had just descended. The rushing water was as bright blue as Champion's eyes and it flowed into a deep pool that bubbled and sprayed at the foot of the falls and then spread out with swirling ripples that lapped at grassy edges. King Jesus dismounted and lifted Bradey to the ground. Champion wandered to the water's edge and stooped his great neck to drink deeply. But the Master took Bradey by the hand and led him to a smooth white rock.

"Climb up there and watch me," he said with a smile. "I'm going to get us a drink of cool, Living Water."

Then, standing tall at the edge of the deep pool, the Master made a smooth gesture that looked like he was scooping a handful of air. Suddenly the water rose before him in the shape of a large pitcher and poured a trickle of water into his cupped hands. He drank deeply as Bradey watched, wide-eyed.

Then he turned with a smile and said, "Hand me your cup." Bradey looked questioningly and lifted his open hands as if to show the King that he had no cup and the

THE LITTLEST WARRIOR

Master chuckled, "Look there; right beside you on the rock."

Bradey glanced sideways and gasped with surprise, for there at his side was a very small golden goblet with a curvy "BJM" engraved on the side. With a giggle of delight, Bradey took the little cup and gave it to King Jesus who filled it with water and handed it back to the happy boy. Bradey didn't think the cup was big enough to satisfy his thirst, but he tipped it and drank the pure, refreshing water, enjoying every drop.

Then he handed it back to the King and asked, "Could I have some more?"

King Jesus laughed with great delight and with a twinkle in his wonderful eyes he answered with a nod toward Bradey's cup.

"You *do* have more; see?" And to Bradey's amazement, he saw that his little goblet was still brimming with water and it spilled over onto his little pink toes as he brought it back to his lips.

"I thought I drank it," he said with a giggle.

"You did! To the last drop," said the Master; "but here in Heaven your cup will always be full. You will always be satisfied because this is a place of abundance where emptiness cannot exist."

Bradey looked into his cup and saw a few sparkling drops left in the bottom; but he knew that the next time he wanted a drink, it would be full again, and all he could think to say was, "Awesome!"

He added his new goblet to the fine collection of gifts in his Miracle Pocket and then sealed it. Champion had sidled up to the white rock so Bradey could climb onto his back. This was the first time he had been allowed to mount up all by himself and he was overcome with glee. Sighing with deep satisfaction as he stroked the curly mane, Bradey could not imagine how God could think of so many wonderful things to put in Heaven; and he touched the petals of his orange rose, remembering his family and wishing he could tell them all about it.

Now the landscape turned into soft, rolling hills and the regal threesome entered a green meadow filled with clumps of tall white lilies that swayed gently to the music of Heaven and filled the air with their perfume. None were crushed beneath the powerful hooves as they passed because wherever Champion stepped the lilies parted to make a path for his feet, as if they were making way for The King and bowing in reverence before Him. Soon they were on the Golden Road again and heading for The Father's House.

The warmth, the light, and the beautiful music had a tranquil effect on the little cherub; and he relaxed his grip on Champion's mane and leaned back against King Jesus as pure peace enveloped him. The closer they got to the mammoth golden gate, the more relaxed he became until he fell asleep in the Master's arms.

Bradey Josheb did not see the court yard filled with worshiping angels; he did not see the crystal mist that shrouded the Father's dwelling place. Bradey slept peacefully as King Jesus approached His Father's Throne; he did not hear the words that passed between them, nor did he see the smiles on their faces. For the time had not come for the inhabitants of this paradise to see God Himself; and yet this little being was engulfed by the strong, sweet presence of the All-Knowing One as King Jesus stood at His Father's right hand with the Littlest Warrior cradled in his arms.

Kids' Paradise

Bradey awoke to the sound of laughter. He felt so warm and calm; loved and protected, even though he did not know exactly where he was. He sat up and rubbed his eyes. Champion was grazing nearby, swishing his beautiful tail, and he looked at Bradey and neighed softly as if to tell him all was well. Bradey sat still, remembering his ride with The Master in every mystical detail. It was like a wonderful dream that he never wanted to forget. He remembered being at The Father's House, too; even though he did not remember what he saw and heard. He knew he was there and he knew that God was pleased to see him. That made him smile. Then he heard the laughter again and looked sideways to an open gate close by. He could see children playing near a sparkling fountain in the middle of a grassy court yard—which Bradey would come to know as the *K.P. Hub*—and King Jesus was right in the middle of them. Bradey got up and walked toward the gate, which was a rainbow of many bright colors. This place was walled by shrubs of variegated green that were covered with sweet-smelling goodies. Bradey knew these blossoms were edible and he picked a fluffy white one to sample. Then he tried a crunchy brown one that was quite tasty, followed by a firm, dark one that melted in his mouth. Having no experience as other children, Bradey could not have understood the joyful pleasure of "snacks", or the resemblance that these heavenly treats bore to childhood favorites of Earth. He had no idea, therefore, that he was sampling celestial versions of marshmallows, graham crackers and chocolate—a Heavenly S'More! He only knew that they were a very great delight and that he had permission to help himself.

THE LITTLEST WARRIOR

Licking his rosy lips, Bradey skipped through the gate and bumped smack-dab into another blonde-haired boy who was taller than him. They both fell with a plop and the tall boy laughed.

"Hi, Bradey; welcome to Kids' Paradise! How did you like my present?"

Bradey remembered him from the reception, but before he could ask, "Who are you, again?" or "What present?" other children were crowding around him and King Jesus was saying, "Come, children! I want you to meet my Littlest Warrior!"

There were children of all shapes and sizes and Bradey was fascinated just looking at his great variety of new friends. There were tall, skinny ones and short, chubby ones; red-heads with freckles and blondies with fair, rosy skin. Three boys with darker skin stood out from the crowd and seemed especially interested in Bradey Josheb. His focus was riveted on them as well, and somehow he knew their names as his brown eyes met theirs.

He reached for them, returning their gleaming smiles and gave them all a man-shake, feeling an instant and powerful connection as he said (quite strongly for such a tot) "'Niko (NEE-ko)...Li (Lee)...Uzi (OO-zee)".

All three beamed with pleasure, feeling very significant and returned an automatic *Squad Nod*, which—unbeknown to these heavenly tykes—was the accepted man-to-man greeting among warriors: a quick, strong nod of acknowledgement accompanied by unwavering eye contact that silently affirmed their devoted

KIDS' PARADISE

comradeship. This gesture of brotherhood was universal in the Heavenly Realm and demonstrated allegiance to the King of Kings and His Cause; but it was especially powerful when exchanged warrior-to-warrior and was often followed by an electric "Victor Volt" from man to man, which these miniature soldiers felt but would not understand until later. They would meet again. The names that had come so easily to Bradey were nicknames; but he would later discover that they were each called away as small children during times of war and persecution on the earth. Now, however, four dimpled cherubs just stood grinning, looking from face to face, until the voice of The Master spoke again.

"Bradey, welcome to Kids' Paradise! This is one of the places in Heaven that I think you will like the most. All of these are my Special Lambs, who were ushered into the heavenlies in their childhood, like you. Each has a special name, a special gift, and a special part in my Master Plan."

Then King Jesus drew Bradey into his arms for one more hug and said in his ear, "I love you, Bradey Josheb, my Littlest Warrior. I will see you again soon. Anchorr will come for you here; but now I want you to spend some time with the children." Then tousling the hair of the boy Bradey had bumped into earlier, he added, "Robert will show you around."

The boys watched in wonder as The Master strode through the Rainbow Gate toward Champion. The majestic steed pranced toward The King and stretched out one leg in front as the other knee touched the ground, bowing low before his Lord. King Jesus mounted smoothly as Champion rose to his feet with a snort. He was ready to go; and they were off so quickly that the boys found themselves blinking at a cloud of gold dust where Jesus and Champion had just stood.

"Awesome!" they said simultaneously, and Robert added in whispered tones of boyish admiration,

"Whenever King Jesus rides off with Champion, they leave a cloud of gold dust!" and then tugging at Bradey's tunic he coaxed him.

"C'mon; you can actually touch it!"

The boys scrambled through the gate to revel in the stuff dreams are made of; but instead of the dirt and dust that would have caused their earthly mothers to douse them in a soapy tub, they stomped their bare, cherub feet in pure powdered gold. They glittered from head to toe as they came back through the Rainbow Gate laughing, tugging, pushing and playing as only little boys can do.

Robert reached for his Miracle Pocket and pulled out a golden goblet with a curvy "RJW" engraved on the side. He tilted his head back and guzzled the Living Water that was spilling over the rim and he had barely finished it when it filled again to the brim. Bradey fumbled at his own Miracle Pocket with his chubby fingers, remembering that he had a goblet, too.

After draining it the first time, Robert pulled him toward the fountain in the center of the courtyard and hollered.

"Taste this!"

Bradey simulated his little mentor and they stretched over the low fountain wall holding their goblets toward the center. Suddenly two center sprays changed their direction and poured the sparkling liquid into the boys' cups. Bradey squealed with delight and pulled it to his lips. It was a little sweeter than Living Water and a bit fizzy; but having no earthly experience with soda pop, it was a brand new taste for Bradey Josheb Markis. Bradey watched again and again as other children ran to the sparkling fountain to get a drink. He was completely amazed each time a towering, fizzy spray would turn from its center position to pour into their cups. There were only seven towers of sparkling water shooting upwards at the center of the fountain, but if more children came with cups the water towers would split into smaller sprays and shoot into every cup, filling them all at once.

Now Robert was off in another direction, making a bee-line for his favorite spot and Bradey scrambled to stay close on his heels. Running down a dusty golden road they came out into a flowered meadow and everywhere Bradey looked there were wispy butterflies, buzzing bumble bees, or dragonflies darting above the wavering blossoms. Robert leaped forward, catching a huge green and purple dragonfly with bulging crimson eyes. Bradey watched breathlessly as he gently touched its fuzzy head, its shiny tail and finally its papery wings.

"They won't fly away," Robert explained. "On Earth they were afraid of us; but up here you can catch anything you want and hold it as long as you like. If you stand still, they will land on you because they like you." Then he laughed out loud, pointing at Bradey's head. "They found you already," he said.

Bradey reached up to rescue a large bumble bee that was stuck in one of his yellow curls and buzzing ferociously. Feeling its furry body in his fingertips,

THE LITTLEST WARRIOR

Bradey lifted it down so he could watch it crawl around on his hands and arms.

"If you did that on earth," Robert exclaimed with arching eyebrows, "they would sting you!" Then, of course, he had to explain *sting* because Bradey had never been stung by a bee. Robert took the opportunity then to tell stories about mosquitoes, spiders and fire ants as well, enjoying every minute of it as his little cousin listened with wide, brown eyes. Then he turned to run again.

"Let's go to the lake!" he hollered over his shoulder; and they ran through the meadow to a place where the long grasses stopped and the ground was covered with fine, white sand. The clear, blue lake was dotted with tiny boats of all sizes that Robert had made, and he lifted one from the water with a grin.

"Take out your boat, Bradey," he said, pointing to the Miracle Pocket. "Let's race!"

Bradey had not had even a minute to think about his presents. But now he remembered the beautiful toy sailboat that was given to him at Celebration Hall. He had not remembered that it was from Robert.

Now, for the first time, Bradey remembered that Robert was in his family and he looked up at him and said, "Are you my cousin?"

"One of them," Robert smiled. "We have lots of cousins on Earth. I made boats for all of them; but I can't give them until they get here. Do you like yours?"

KIDS' PARADISE

Bradey fingered the blue letters on the shiny, white boat. He gently touched the billowy sails and the tiny golden ropes coiled on the bronze deck.

"I love it," he said, "especially these little ropes. I like ropes."

Robert explained all the pieces to him and told him what everything was for. Then he told him all about boats on the earth: sailboats, motor boats, fishing boats, cargo ships, kayaks, canoes, rafts and aircraft carriers. Bradey asked Robert how he knew so much about boats.

Robert said, "I guess 'cuz it's one of my special gifts; King Jesus took me to his Boat House on the Sea of Glass. I'm learning to make boats and sails and fishing nets from two of his best friends named Peter and Paul. Some day I will be a Master Craftsman like them. I don't know what all the boats are for yet, but it sure is fun; plus, I get to play in the water all the time and float all the boats that I make!"

After playing in the clear blue lake for some time and floating all the boats and having races, Robert showed Bradey the Family Dock. It was a special wooden dock that had all the names of the children in Robert's family engraved around the edges. Beside each name was a small post where that child could dock their little boat. Of course, Bradey was very curious about all the names, so Robert told as much as he could about each of them. Bradey especially enjoyed the part about his brothers, because Robert had known each of them on earth before he was called away, and they laughed together about the stories that Robert remembered. Suddenly Bradey noticed a shiny, silver arc that touched the end of the dock and curved upwards high into the sky and then down again toward the water, stopping in mid air about six feet above the lake.

"What's that, Robert?" he asked.

"A water slide!" Robert answered enthusiastically. "Follow me!" Then, hanging his tunic on a nearby peg, he scampered up the silver stairs—which Bradey had not noticed until Robert began his climb. Soon Robert stood at the top of the silver arc.

Bradey hung his own tunic on a peg, as there was a tidy row of them at the base of the slide, checking to make sure his orange rose was carefully sheathed and his Miracle Pocket was still on his belt. Noticing his gleaming white shorts with gold trim for the first time, he decided they were very convenient for times like this and he patted his little round belly, investigating with one finger the funny little "button" in the center of it. It tickled so he giggled out loud.

Now Robert called to him from the top.

"Hurry up, Bradey! I'm waiting to show you how to do it!"

As Bradey clambered a bit awkwardly toward the top he noticed how long and slender Robert's belly was and wondered why his own was so round; he also wondered if Robert had a "button"; but then he looked down at the lake and forgot everything else.

From the high steps of the silver arc he saw something he had not seen from the shore: beautifully colored creatures of all shapes and sizes moving about in the crystal blue water, and soft, curious plants growing on the bottom.

Reaching the top where Robert stood, Bradey pointed at the scene below and quizzed him, "Robert! What are those?"

"My fish and stuff; my lake is called *Aquarium* because all my favorite fish are in here, and I have some pretty big ones. They're waiting for us at the bottom!"

Then, he landed with a jolly *THUMP* on his heavenly bottom and went whizzing down the silver slide with animated shouts and both arms in the air.

Disappearing into the cool water with a wonderful splash that spewed a fountain of rainbow colors, Robert bobbed to the surface just in time to swing himself onto the back of something smooth and gray. Bradey followed suit and was soon shooting down the slide at a speed that whipped the curls around his face and filled his chest with dizzy delight. With lightening speed he hit the water and bobbed to the top, sputtering and squealing all at once.

"Get on!" Robert nodded toward another gray blob next to Bradey; but since he had never seen a dolphin, he wasn't quite sure what to do. As he looked at it and touched it cautiously, Robert said, "Help him, Jets!" and before Bradey could blink the dolphin had ducked between his chubby legs and surfaced with Bradey on his back. Bradey was so surprised that the shock on his face made Robert laugh.

"These are my pet dolphins, Sub and Jets. I named them that because they can take you under like a submarine or pull you like a Jet Ski. Aren't they cool? They will take us wherever we want to go. Let's go to the bottom and see some of my fish; down, Sub!"

Robert disappeared beneath the water but it was so clear that Bradey could see him on Sub's back swimming below. He watched with fascination but wasn't sure if he wanted to do the same thing. Suddenly Sub bolted for the top and dove into the air as Robert yelled, "Wahoo" at the top of his lungs.

Landing with a colorful splash, Robert said, "You have to tell them what to do; here, I'll help you this time." With a short leap, Robert sat snugly on Jets' back behind Bradey with one arm protectively around his little middle.

"The works, Jets!" he commanded and the pet dolphin took off like a motor boat across Lake Aquarium. The boys whooped and hollered with glee as Jets leaped and twirled. He sashayed on the surface, jumped and dropped, and lunged up and down, skipping across the lake like a tossed rock. Bradey's favorite maneuver was the High-jump Freefall where Jets leaped high into the air and crashed with a loud belly flop that splashed wonderful colors in all directions. Suddenly Jets decided that Bradey's initiation should go to the next level, and Robert sensed it.

He tightened his grip on Bradey's middle and shouted, "Hang on, we're goin' under!"

Jets jumped higher than ever and did a nosedive into the lake, plunging to the bottom where he slowed to a smooth cruise so Bradey could take in the sites. What Bradey did not realize because he had not experienced swimming on Earth, was that he didn't have to hold his breath under the water. He could breathe and laugh and even talk to Robert—except it sounded a little different, of course—and there were lots of bubbles.

Bradey pointed to a very curious "fish" that peered at them from the mouth of a coral cave.

"That's T.C., my octopus," Robert bubbled. "He's the guardian of all my treasure chests."

Jets parked outside the cave and the boys glided in. There was a soft, glowing green light that made T.C.'s purple, spotty skin look a bit psychedelic. He was hovering over a mound of small, gemstone boxes. Robert lifted one of T.C.'s large, squirmy tentacles and placed it over his shoulders.

"Share, T.C." he ordered audaciously.

The big octopus slid back so the boys could dig through the treasure boxes. Some were carved from black onyx stone and hinged with silver (Robert declared that these were for the boys) and others were carved from pearl and hinged with gold—for the girls, Robert said. Choosing a triangular black onyx box for himself, Bradey then picked up a beautiful pearl one and asked if he could take it, too. He was not quite sure why he needed a girl's treasure chest, but he felt very certain about it, so Robert grinned broadly and heartily agreed. Mounting Jets, they waved to T.C. and Bradey laughed when his new creature-friend actually grinned and waved back with at least five of his eight arms!

Once again on the surface, Jets landed onshore and the boys flopped out on the white sand to Son themselves in the Light of the Lamb. Later as they headed back toward the K.P. Hub along the dusty, golden Kids' Paradise Parkway, Bradey was filled with even more excitement and anticipation to see all the other places Robert was describing to him. He looked forward to getting a grand tour of them: Cloud House was a menagerie of playful activities like jump-houses, gymnastics, indoor sports and games; Ark Acres was the heavenly equivalent of a zoo and wildlife preserve; Cosmos Mountain was an exciting place for outdoor sports and adventures like rock-climbing, cliff-diving, surfing and parasailing (even flying!); and TykeTech Learning Laboratory was the fascinating location for all things creative, scientific and technological. He also mentioned the Great Hall of Music, Sir Betters Bakery and, of course, the Birthday Party Palace.

Robert told Bradey about the frequent visits from King Jesus, who loved spending time with His children. He explained that all the children get lots of attention from The Master, their angelic Guardians, and their assigned mentors who are training them for kingdom business of all kinds.

"But its not like chores," he clarified, "because everything is fun and there's nothing up here you don't want to do." (Then, of course, he had to explain *chores*!)

As Bradey's head spun with the thrills of Kid's Paradise, he and Robert got drinks from the fountain and plopped down on the silky grass of the K.P. Hub to rest. A group of girls came by with trays from Sir Betters Bakery. They were stacked with wonderful delights that Bradey gobbled with gusto; never realizing of course, that these were the eternally enriched versions of chocolate chip cookies, Rice Krispy treats, and frosted brownies.

"I guess God thought of everything when he built this place," Bradey sighed with contentment, closing his eyes and savoring every memory of this wonderful spot for kids in The Master's Heaven.

A boisterous chuckle above him made his eyes pop open suddenly. "This ain't the half of it, Bud," laughed a bronze-skinned boy with a shock of straight platinum hair poking this way and that from under a curious hat. He lounged on the fat branch of a wide, leafy tree above Bradey's head.

Bradey sat up and smiled, instantly deciding that climbing trees was a wonderful idea. In a flash he was up on the branch with his new friend who said,

"Hi, Bradey. I'm Reece Ryder, but my buds call me *Ryder*, 'cuz I'm usually on horseback. I'm going with you to The Royal Corrals; Anchorr and Hagan will be here any minute."

Bradey was filled with new enthusiasm all over again about going on another adventure. Reece Ryder looked down at Robert and swung off the branch, landing beside him. This was when Bradey noticed the black and gold boots.

"Hey, Skipper!" Ryder said with a freckled grin, giving Robert a man-shake and adding, "how's my boatin' buddy?"

"Hey, Cowboy! Where ya been? When are you taking me on another ride?"

"On a crock or a stallion?" Ryder laughed, tousling Robert's hair. "I'll be back; gotta show Bradey around the corrals. Later, dude!"

THE LITTLEST WARRIOR

Suddenly Bradey was lifted from the tree branch by the powerful arms of Anchorr. And as they went through the Rainbow Gate with Reece Ryder and his Guardian, Hagan, Bradey turned and waved at Robert, gleefully adding a new phrase to his collection of boy words, "Later, dude!"

Champion Ranch

The Light of the Lamb was warm and bright upon Bradey Josheb as the foursome walked down the golden road. Anchorr had Bradey high upon his left shoulder so his short little legs wouldn't wear out trying to keep up. Ryder had skipped up ahead and was picking Living Twigs from his favorite trees and filling his shirt pocket with stray gemstones that he found along the side of the road. Bradey watched him with curious interest, noticing the shiny boots again, and his black and gold hat. He wanted to play with Ryder but he knew Anchorr and Hagan were on a mission because their long strides were covering a lot of ground. Anchorr spoke to him, "Bradey, have you met Hagan? He is Ryder's guardian. He was allowed to stay in Heaven when Reece was called away because he is currently assigned at Champion Ranch where the King's horses are attended and trained for service."

"Awesome!" Bradey beamed. "Are we going there now?"

"Yes, we are," answered Anchorr, giving Hagan a grinning glance that smacked of wonderful secrets. Bradey did not know what was in store for him, but he was very excited and stretched his chubby neck to see ahead.

"Anchorr, what's a 'cowboy'? … and what does *skipper* mean?"

Anchorr chuckled as he answered, for he was continually pleased with Bradey's character qualities.

"You are very observant," he affirmed. "You heard Robert and Reece call each other by their nicknames. In Kids' Paradise, the children enjoy giving special names to each other that represent one of their gifts from the Master. They call Robert 'skipper' because of his skill with boats: it is a name for a boat captain. They call Reece 'cowboy' because that is a name for someone who works with livestock, and Reece is very skilled with the Master's steeds."

"Cool!" Bradey exclaimed, using another new word he had picked up from Kids' Paradise. "What do you think mine will be?"

"You are a warrior," Anchorr stated with angelic pleasure. "But your nickname is something the Master allows your peers to assign—the people who will work the closest with you. So we will both have to wait and see."

Ryder had turned off the Golden Road and disappeared into the trees. As Bradey and the two guardians rounded the bend, the site took Bradey's breath away. They stepped through a massive gate made of huge logs. They were not bare, as logs used for building on Earth, but covered with copper bark and hinged with pure gold. A sign at the top made of black onyx, pearl and turquoise said **"Welcome to Champion Ranch, Home of the King's Chargers"**.

Before them lay a beautiful valley of long, silky, grass that swayed in the heavenly breeze. A wide pathway of white stone followed a crystal blue bubbling brook that wound through the valley to a place in the center where there was some kind of commotion going on. Beyond it were some hills in a half-moon shape that graduated into some big mountains covered with vibrant evergreens. Their distant peaks were snow-capped and seemed to touch the pink and gold clouds that hung in Heaven's sky. If Bradey had known how many mountain men were in his earthly bloodline, maybe he would have understood the reason for the thumping of his tiny heart. But all he knew was that he was very excited to learn everything about this place, and to somehow get to the tops of those mountains!

Ryder was calling him now, "'ey, Bradey! C'mon, mate; the corrals are just ahead!"

He was pointing to the area where Bradey had heard all the commotion, and gold dust was hovering in the air above something that looked like a big circle. As they came closer, Bradey saw that it was a round fence—although he didn't exactly know what a fence was—that was made of the same copper logs as the gate. Now Bradey saw that there were a few Guardians standing around the edges and some men in the center with some big horses. These men were wearing the same curious hats that Ryder had, and Bradey was wondering what it all meant.

Anchorr lifted Bradey down from his shoulder and set him into a curious seat on top of a fence post. Bradey did not know what the seat was but it was a copper color, like the fence, and padded with soft, plush blue like Champion's red velvet coverlet. He looked around the corral and noticed that there were several of these perched upon the fence where little tykes like him could sit and watch the goings on. They were slightly curved in the middle with a golden handle at the front to hold on to. Straps hanging from each side had silver loops at the bottom to put your feet in, and as soon as Bradey touched the golden handle (which was actually a saddle horn) the straps shortened automatically so his feet

THE LITTLEST WARRIOR

slipped snugly into the loops. Ryder hopped up on the fence beside him to explain.

"These are saddles, like we used on Earth. That's the saddle horn and these are stirrups for your feet. We'd put these on the backs of our horses to make the ridin' a bit easier; but we don't need 'em in Heaven, so up here they just use 'em as seats for old times' sake." Then, climbing into another saddle close by, Ryder hollered, "Ride em' cowboy! Let's watch the rodeo!"

Bradey saw the men in the center working with some beautiful horses. They stroked their powerful necks, led them around with golden ropes and even mounted up and made them do all sorts of things while they rode them around the corral. Bradey was fascinated, watching the "cowboys" work with the horses. He supposed they were cowboys because they were working with the Master's horses and all of them were dressed like Ryder; except they had silky, white shirts with fringes on the back in a 'V' from the shoulders and a bit of silky fringe along the forearm near the cuffs. They were also wearing a heavenly version of Levi jeans, black with copper stitching and a large golden monogram of "CR" on the back pocket. Their belts were gold and the buckles were pearl; and even though Bradey was too young to understand all these details, he sure thought they looked "cool" in their cowboy duds. Anchorr and Hagan watched the boys with great satisfaction. Being heavenly guardians of the Most High and assigned to warriors throughout the ages of mankind, they knew what it took to be chosen for this honor. Therefore, it was very pleasurable for them to see the character and interests of true warriors blossoming from within these cherub hearts. Anchorr bent low to speak in Bradey's ear.

"These are the Royal Corrals of Champion Ranch. The Master has given your grandfathers the privilege of working with his stallions, along with others who are gifted in the same way. These are the white horses that will one day carry the Saints of the Most High in the Last Battle when the King of Kings leads them to victory over the arch enemy, Satan. If you will look up at the hills around the ranch, you will see thousands of these white horses. They come into the corrals a few at a time to work with these men. Their training and care are very important; and your grandfathers are gifted to do it well."

Bradey was peering intensely through the gold dust now, looking for his grandfathers, so he had not noticed the person coming toward him leading a beautiful white pony.

"Well, Bradey! Glad to see you made it! Me an' Grandpa Doc have been waitin' for ya!" It was Great-grandpa Gail. He removed one golden glove to reach up and pinch Bradey on the cheek. "Look what I brought ya!"

Bradey was speechless as he stared at the pure white pony. He had crystal blue eyes, just like Champion. His mane and tale were thick and soft, but kind of short. *I guess he's a cherub,* Bradey thought, *a little one, like me.* Bradey remembered King Jesus telling him that he would have his very own horse, but he thought he had to be a big warrior first. He was overcome with delight and squealed joyfully, clapping his chubby hands, "Is he mine, Grampa? Did King Jesus give him to me?"

"He sure did," Grandpa chuckled. "Do you like him?"

"I *love* him! What's his name?"

THE LITTLEST WARRIOR

Anchorr answered the question. "You will decide when the time is right. The warrior and his steed are one in battle; you must choose carefully."

Just then, Greater-grandpa Doc came up and raised his pointer finger in the air saying, "Yessirree, Bradey Boy. An, that ain't all; lookee here."

He carried two golden boxes and lifted them now for Bradey to open the lids. Inside one box was a tiny pair of black and gold cowboy boots; and inside the other was a black and gold cowboy hat that said, *Champion Ranch* on the band. One grandpa slipped Bradey's boots on his little pink feet and the other grandpa topped him off with the hat, both chuckling with glee.

"Am I a cowboy?" Bradey giggled, which brought peals of laughter from the grandfathers and Reece Ryder.
"Well, not exactly," Great-grandpa Gail answered with a big grin. "But we want ya to look like one whenever you visit the ranch. So these will be in the Heavenly Tack Barn on yer own personal peg; and you can put them on every time you come. Now come on down here and try out yer pony."

With that Great Grandpa lifted Bradey from his perch in the saddle-seat.

"Can he carry me?" Bradey quizzed, "...since he's just a cherub-hoss?"

This brought more laughter from the grandfathers and Greater-grandpa Doc chuckled, "He-Heeee! Well, so are you an' I reckon that's a purty good match."

With that Bradey was placed on the back of his new pony and Ryder chimed in, "Get out yer rope, Mate; this is what it's for!"

So Bradey reached into his Miracle Pocket and drew out his gold, silver, and copper coil. Great-grandpa showed him how to place it gently around his pony's neck and tie a special knot. Then he took off the lead line he had used to bring the pony out, and said, "Take him for a ride, cowboy!"

"Go, Cherub!" Bradey nudged him timidly between the ears, quivering with excitement. Other cowboys had joined the onlookers and they all erupted into gales of laughter now, enjoying the show. Ryder hopped from his perch on the fence and took over for the time being, deciding to teach Bradey a thing or two.

"It's okay to call 'im *Cherub* until he's ready for 'is <u>real</u> name, Bradey. Now, just tap him real careful on the sides with your boots whenever you say *Go* so he'll learn what the word means. Horses are very smart in Heaven; they learn what you mean really quick and they always obey their masters. If you want 'im to turn <u>this</u> way, touch 'is neck right here; and if you want 'im to turn <u>that</u> way, touch 'is neck right there. Got it?"

"Umm, *you betcha*," Bradey answered, picking up a new expression from the grandfathers.

He didn't quite understand but he was very comfortable and very ready to ride his pony. He touched him gently on the sides of his belly with the golden heels of his new black boots and Cherub lurched forward a few steps, jostling Bradey precariously to the left. Grandpa Gail stepped to the rescue and sat Bradey upright once again, then whispered in Cherub's ear, as he patted his furry white neck.

"Don't wait for *me*, now; you listen to Bradey Josheb; he's your new master."

From the pocket of his silky white shirt, Grandpa Gail drew a couple of Golden Nibbles and put them under the colt's nose. He gobbled them happily and began to walk. Bradey tried turning him this way and that, talking to his little "hoss" all the while. Then suddenly Bradey tapped him a little too aggressively with his boots and Cherub jumped and began to trot. Ryder saw Bradey slipping to one side and ran to catch up with them, but didn't make it in time and Bradey fell with a thump on the ground. Bradey was very surprised to find himself so quickly on the ground and he looked up with wide, brown eyes, then got the giggles and began to laugh. Of course, nothing hurts in heaven, so the ground felt like landing on a featherbed, except Bradey was covered in gold dust. Bradey saw that Cherub was standing patiently nearby, watching him, his lead rope dragging the ground.

"Call 'im to come, Matey!" Ryder encouraged as he pulled Bradey to his feet and snatched up his new hat which had bounced off his head when he'd hit the ground. Plopping it firmly atop Bradey's yellow curls, he said, "Remember to tap 'im *real soft* with your boots; he's jist a baby."

"Come, Cherub," Bradey called to his pony, clapping his chubby pink hands together. The little colt came quickly to his side and Ryder boosted him up on Cherub's back, handing him the rope.

"Now, make 'im go once 'round the corral and then take 'im over to that golden trough under the fountain. He'll need a nice, cool drink after you work 'im. I'll be there waitin' for you, and we'll give 'im a treat for doin' a good job."

So Bradey set off once again around the corral, being careful this time to tap Cherub's sides very gently with his little black boots. The pony walked obediently, listening to Bradey's commands. He even turned him in a full circle and made him go the other way, which drew a round of hearty cheers from the group of cowboy and angelic spectators.

"Atta boy, Bradey!" shouted Great-grandpa Gail, and Greater-grandpa Doc chimed out.

"You bet yer boots, Bradey-boy! Make the little feller work for ya!" The grandfathers were having a great time leaning on the fence and watching the "Cherub Rodeo".

Then Bradey turned Cherub toward the fountain and said, "Are you ready for a drink? Let's go!"

But Bradey had not learned how to keep his horse reined in; so when Cherub saw the fountain and set off lickety-split to get his drink, Bradey did not know how to slow him down.

"Wait! Not so fast! Stop, Cher-rubub-ub-ub!" he squealed as his heavenly bottom endured a good bouncing all across the corral to the other side.

The grandfathers began to run after them, and Ryder—who was waiting at the fountain—saw what was coming and just got out of the way. Cherub slowed to a trot, which did not help Bradey regain his balance, and stopped short in front of the trough to lean forward for a long drink of Living Water. Poor little Bradey had not had a chance to get his bearings and he toppled right over Cherub's fuzzy head and landed with a splash in the horses' watering trough! Greater-grandpa Doc dipped a powerful hand into the ripples and pulled Bradey out of the water and into his arms in one swoop.

"Whatcha doin' Bradey-boy? It's a waterin' trough, not a swimmin' hole!" And all the cowboys burst into guffaws as the very startled and totally soaked cherub cowboy gasped for air and rubbed his eyes, grinning from ear to ear.

"That was fun!" he burbled, water dripping from his chin, as Grandpa Gail pulled off his boots to dump the water out and Ryder rescued his cowboy hat that was still floating in the trough. Bradey was wet long enough to get cooled off from his ride; but since there is no misery in Heaven, he was soon dry and comfy in the sweet, warm Light of the Lamb.

"Time for treats!" chirped Ryder, heading for the Heavenly Tack Barn.

Bradey was right on his heels, not wanting to miss a thing. Just inside the door was a softly-woven replica of an earthly gunny sack full of Golden Nibbles, the heavenly horse treat. Cherub had trotted happily behind the boys, knowing where they were headed, and was nudging Bradey's neck with his silky-soft nose before he could thrust a chubby hand into the bag and come out with a fist full of pony treats. Ryder showed him how to hold his hand flat and let Cherub nibble from his palm. It tickled so much that Bradey giggled and giggled as his furry little colt relished in the delectable treats.

Two boys approached Bradey and Cherub with broad grins.

"'ey, fellas." Ryder welcomed each of them with a man-shake. "Bradey, these are my mates: Toby Jasper and Tate Marshall! They were both slaves on Earth; in different countries, and hundreds of years apart; but they were very good stable boys to some mean and cruel masters who didn't deserve them. So King Jesus brought them home and gave them a special place in the Royal Corrals. They get to take care of Champion himself!"

"Awesome!" Bradey said, as they stooped slightly to receive his cherub man-shake.

Bradey could tell by Toby's shining black face and Tate's happy, freckled one that these boys would be his good friends, or "mates" as Ryder called them. He smiled at them, showing deep dimples as Toby ruffled his yellow curls and grinned back.

"Welcome to the Master's Heaven, Bradey. There ain't no better place for boys to be!"

Then Bradey noticed the curious tools they were carrying and asked, "What are those?"

"Brushes," they both answered together, laughing.

"We brush Champion every day when he returns to the corrals; and after he's all groomed, we get on his back and he gives us a ride to the top of the mountain!" Tate beamed.

Bradey shivered from tip to toes, remembering his own fantastic ride with the King to Mount Witness and Mount Imminent. He wanted to follow Toby and Tate and watch them groom Champion, but just then Bradey was swooshed off his feet into Great-grandpa Gail's arms again.

"Later, Mates!" he hollered as his grandfather carted him off.

"Let yer ol' grandpa show ya somethin'," he grinned, sauntering across the barn to a row of copper pegs along one wall. They stopped in front of a peg that was much lower than the rest and Grandpa Gail put Bradey down so he could see it straight on.

"This is where ya hang yer hat," he said proudly, "an that's where I hang mine," he added, pointing upwards to a higher peg next to Bradey's spot.

Bradey had not even realized that he had been "cowboying" around in his boots, hat and cherub tunic until he saw his jeans and tasseled shirt hanging on his peg! He glanced down at his little angel robe, with dimpled, pink knees peeking out between its hem and his boot tops, and raised his eyebrows at the grandfathers, which threw them into gales of laughter once again.

"You can wear 'em next time," Grandpa Gail told him, removing Bradey's hat to ruffle his curls. "This time ya had to break in yer boots!"

Bradey hung his hat and his braided rope on the peg with his cowboy clothes and sat down on his own little bench to take off his boots. Ryder was calling him, as he stashed them neatly under the little bench for next time.

"C'mon, Bradey! You can sit on the haystack, Mate; an' watch me work Prince Kye."

Then Ryder hopped up on the fence and gave a peculiar whistle, which fascinated Bradey because he had not learned how to whistle yet. He followed the direction of Ryder's eyes and saw a fine horse lift its majestic head from the grazing herd on the hillside. Ryder whistled again and the steed whinnied in response and reared into the air. Making his way through the herd, he was soon galloping down the hillside toward The Royal Corrals.

Ryder had already told Bradey about naming his horse. 'Kye' meant *"like the sea"* and Ryder had explained that his earthly home in Australia was *"beside some beautiful water, sort of like Robert's Lake Aquarium"*; and that he had loved the sea and played there all the time, looking for *chrysocolla.* This was a gemstone found in the region by miners, but Ryder had never found one himself. He had always loved the one that his mother wore on a silver chain around her neck. It was shades of mixed blue and green, just like Kye's big beautiful eyes; so Ryder had named his horse after his beloved sea and his mother's gemstone.

That's when he had told Bradey of his "special spot"; one that King Jesus had given him at the foot of the sloping hills. Bradey had asked him what he was going to do with his Living Twigs and Ryder had answered, "Plant them in my Special Spot". Then he had described it to Bradey, who had hung on every word. He said there was a blue-green pond full of lily-pads with fat, singing frogs on them; and tall cat-tails where

THE LITTLEST WARRIOR

birds trilled back and forth to each other. Ryder said that he and Prince Kye loved to go there for quiet times to gaze at the beauty of Heaven and watch sparkly green, blue, and silver lizards scamper across the rocks to the water's edge. Bradey was remembering all these amazing things that Ryder had told him, just as Prince Kye came snorting into the corral and trotted up to his little master. Ryder slipped the lead around Kye's neck and led him over to the haystack to meet Bradey. Bradey was all smiles as he petted Kye's soft, flowing mane, and he noticed that there was a large, flat blue-green stone hanging on a silver ribbon around his neck. This must be the gemstone Ryder told him about. Bradey was glad his buddy had found one in Heaven. Then Bradey looked into Prince Kye's beautiful blue-green eyes, thinking he had seen them somewhere before, but not quite remembering that one of The Brothers had eyes a lot like that.

Soon Ryder was in the center of the corral, working his magnificent steed, and Bradey was curled up on the Heavenly Haystack watching his every move with great delight. Now, even cherubs need a little nap now and then, and after Bradey's exciting adventures at The Royal Corral his little eyelids were feeling heavy. Before long the twitching of his round, pink toes became still and his head nodded deeply a time or two; but though he struggled to stay awake, the Littlest Warrior was soon curled up in the soft celestial hay, fast asleep, and dreaming of being all grown up and riding over the hills on his wonderful horse with Reece Ryder and Prince Kye close behind.

Bradey stirred only slightly when a pair of large hands gently lifted him from the Heavenly Haystack; but right away he was snuggled into a large, warm something that felt soft and silky, and a bit cushy—enough to lull him right back into the dreamy land of napping cherubs. Unbeknown to Bradey, he was sitting backwards on Greater Grandfather's horse, leaning forward onto his grandpa's torso, and feeling the white silk of the cowboy shirt against his very accommodating chubby cheek. The swaying loppity-lop of the horse's unhurried pace relaxed his pudgy little body even more, causing him to slide lower on Grandpa Doc's lap into a very comfortable heap…

…A warm, gentle breeze caressed Bradey's curls, and the musical warble of a singing bird caused him to stir and open his eyes. He noticed that he was lying on a very soft pillow, and that a small matching blanket covered his feet and legs. Although he didn't really *know* what blankets and pillows were he snuggled into them both deciding that, whatever they were and wherever they came from, they were very comforting and reminded him of his mother. His droopy eyes closed again and, wondering if she was doing better now, he reached down to his belt to feel for his orange rose. In his dreamy state, he fingered the crystal teardrops on the stem, and wished he could tell his mom that he was happy and that everything was going to be alright. Subconsciously, his little fingers felt for the Mother's Kiss on his forehead and he remembered

THE LITTLEST WARRIOR

King Jesus telling him to call, and that He would answer; so under his sweet, baby breath he whispered his desire, ever so sincerely.

"King Jesus, please make sure my mother is happy. Could you send those angels again; just in case she needs them?"

The breeze began to stir in the garden and the singing of the birds swelled into the air like a joyous choir. Bradey smiled, knowing that angels had been dispatched through the portal and that they would hover around his mother and take very good care of her—since he wasn't there to do it himself!

He opened his eyes then, and looked ahead, lying still but glancing about. He was no longer in the Royal Corral sleeping on the hay, but was in a very beautiful place full of trees and flowers, with butterflies winging their way from blossom to blossom. Bradey blinked with sleepy satisfaction, recognizing some dragonflies like the ones that Robert had shown him at Lake Aquarium, and some fuzzy bumblebees. He smiled happily, enjoying this peaceful place—whatever it was—when suddenly a very speedy little something came whizzing past his head. It was shiny like a dragonfly, fluttering like a butterfly, but darting here and there so quickly that he could hardly keep track of it!

Bradey sat up, following the little creature around the garden with his eyes, and rubbing a crease on his face where his new pillow had left its mark. He was on a covered, swinging garden bench with soft cushions on the seat and the back. He kicked his feet to make it move a little and looked up at the canopy above his head. It was sheer and billowing, letting the Light of

A GRANDMOTHER'S GARDEN

the Lamb come through to touch the cherubs upturned face.

Catching movement from the corner of his eye, Bradey glanced sideways and saw Greater-grandpa Doc coming across a verdant green lawn from the arched doorway of a darling cottage surrounded by rose bushes. He was carrying two tumblers of something pinkish-yellow that looked very cool and good to drink.

"Well, hello there, Bradey-boy!" Grandpa chuckled. "There's nothin' like a good nap, don't ya know! Yer gramma's fixed us some nice cool lemonade!" he added, handing him the smaller of the two crystal glasses.

"Yum!" Bradey responded with glee, grinning briefly, but remembering the speedy critter and adding with a groggy croak in his voice, "Grandpa Doc, what's that?"

He tried to point it out but it wouldn't stay still long enough to let them focus on it.

"Why, that's a hummin'bird! Yessiree! Jist hold out one finger in front of you, this-a-way Bradey, an' that little critter'll fly right over here an' let ya look at 'im!"

So Bradey held out a fat pointer finger and, in a flash, the hummingbird was perched there, breathing hard but sitting still. The cherub giggled with excitement and piped, "Does he like lemonade, Grampa?"

"I reckon he does," Grandpa chuckled. "Tip yer glass a bit and let 'im have a sip."

THE LITTLEST WARRIOR

Bradey tipped his little glass a bit too far and the lemonade sloshed out on his knee; but it wasn't a problem of course, because there are no sticky messes in Heaven. The tiny bird dipped its beak in the glass and then shook its head furiously and ruffled its feathers.

"He-heeee! Can ya beat that? It's too sour for the little fella. I told yer Gran'mama to put a little more sugar in there but acourse she wouldn't hear of it," he added, slapping his knee with amusement.

"Why, Doc, don't be silly!" came a voice close by, "You know you can step right over there and get it from the lemon tree if ya don't like my recipe!"

"Now, now, Dearie; don't fret. I'm jist a-kiddin' ya;" then winking at Bradey, Grandpa Doc whispered, "Cain't imagine why she still makes lemonade anymore when she can git it ready-made from the lemon tree. But I'm sure glad she makes them cookies!"

Bradey looked up to see a round, smiling grandmother with soft brown hair and hazel eyes bending over with a plate of warm cookies to offer him a treat. The hummingbird flitted back to his garden adventures and Bradey reached for a cookie and took such a big bite that a very melty chocolate chip ended up on the tip of his nose. The grandmother chuckled and wiped it with a corner of her apron. Then she took his face in her hands and, seeing the silvery keepsake on his forehead, whispered softly.

"Oh…your Mother's Kiss; how sweet." Then she kissed him soundly on the cheek and added, "I'm your Great-great Grandma Hazel. Welcome to my garden, Bradey!"

She put the plate of cookies on a nearby table and sat down beside Bradey on the garden swing, giving him a comfy squeeze around the shoulders. When she sat, she pushed a little with her feet to put the swing in motion and Bradey giggled with delight.

"Do you like my swing?" she chortled.

"Why, 'course he does!" Grandpa Doc answered abruptly. "Ain't a boy nowheres that don't like a swing. Ain't that right, Bradey!"

And Grandpa reached out one leg and gave the swing another shove with his boot, setting Grandma off balance and making Bradey squeal with delight.

"That'll do, Doc;" Grandma Hazel chided sweetly, trying not to chuckle. "You'll make 'im spill his lemonade."

"Well, that don't matter up here, Hazel; might as well enjoy the fun," his eyes twinkled as he sat back in his chair and tipped his glass to finish off his lemonade, which reminded Bradey to take a drink of his own.

"How do you like the blanket and pillow I made for you, Bradey?" Grandma Hazel asked as she picked up the little quilt and folded it neatly into her lap with the pillow on top.

He looked up at her with big, brown eyes, licking his rosy lips between cookie bites and quizzed, "You can *make* things?...all by yourself?"

"Why, sure, sweetheart," she chuckled. "Everybody can; God put a little bit of His creativity in all of us."

THE LITTLEST WARRIOR

"He *did*?" Bradey responded with amazement. "What can *I* make, Gramma Hazel?"

"Well, I don't know," she chuckled again, patting his chubby leg; "but there's no hurry because you've got lots of time to find out!"

She and Grandpa Doc laughed out loud then and he added, "Ain't that the truth!"

Then Grandpa Doc stood up and said, "You've about finished off that lemonade, Bradey-boy. Wha'-da-ya say we go try out the lemon tree?"

Bradey was off the garden swing in a flash and running across the soft grass in his bare feet. Grandpa followed him while Grandma reached for a large, guiltless cookie and settled into her swing, enjoying the scene. Taking a dainty bite, and responding with a subconscious, "Mmmm," she glanced at her smooth, beautiful hands and remembered how worn they had become on earth before her journey had ended. She looked up at Bradey, standing on his tiptoes to reach the lemon tree spout, Grandpa's big hands open and ready to give him a boost, but opting for the satisfaction of watching him do it himself—knowing he wanted to. Grandma chuckled, remembering the joy of caring for her own children on earth, and feeling very pleased to have another little one tottering around in her garden.

After the lemonade adventure, Grandpa and Bradey came back for another cookie and Grandma enthusiastically suggested that they go for a stroll and show Bradey around the garden. Grandma took great delight in showing Bradey her favorite flowers, while Grandpa Doc kept a wary eye open for the garden critters. Bradey touched the roses, smelled the lilacs and honeysuckle, played in the fountain pond with a mother duck and her eight fuzzy ducklings, and dried his feet on the spongy, green moss. He chased butterflies, but Grandma showed him how to stand still and let them come to him. Grandpa found a big tortoise who stoically demonstrated his ability to pull his head and legs into his shell, which brought peals of cherubic laughter from Bradey. For the first time, he experienced the boyish delights of touching everything in sight; from the clammy green gecko to the fluffy long-eared baby bunny rabbit, which he could not bear to part with and so, carried around nestled in his chubby arms.

Grandpa Doc was just up ahead, peering through the Rose of Sharon hedge that bordered a Wisteria trellis hanging over a dainty white gate.

Bradey was instantly intrigued. "Look, Grandma! Grandpa Doc found a gate!"

Chuckling at the cherub's sense of adventure, she cooperated, "Why, he sure did. Where do you s'pose it leads?" Soon they were all standing at the little gate looking into another beautiful garden. It was beautiful like Grandma Hazel's, but had lots of stone walls and curving paths that made it seem very mysterious and exciting. As Bradey looked at the end of one path, wondering where it went, a big white tiger with black stripes ambled around the bend and stopped, blinking at the onlookers. Soon another one came into view and Bradey recognized them as Ebony and Alabaster, the tigers that had brought in the cake at his Grand Reception.

THE LITTLEST WARRIOR

"Grandpa!" Bradey shouted energetically. "It's Ebony and Alabaster, from the party! Is this where they live?"

"Sure as I'm standin' here!" Grandpa chuckled. "Looks like they et up the rest of that cake, though!"

"Come, Ebony! Come, Alabaster!" Bradey coaxed, reaching over the gate. "Can we go in?"

"Not yet, honey." Grandma Hazel said. "The tigers will come to you; but we can't go in the garden because the person it was created for isn't here yet. When your Grandma ZeZe gets to Heaven, you can come and see it; but right now her tigers and her peacocks, Turq and Coral, live there and mind the four gates until she arrives."

This information opened a floodgate of questions from Bradey that the double-great grandparents answered cheerfully and with great amusement, marveling at the phenomenal expansion of this cherub's little heavenly mind; for they remembered how long it took on the earth for little ones to learn and grow. He told them he saw Grandma ZeZe through the portal and sang the *Happy Birthday* song to her at the celebration. He reminded them that his Grandma ZeZe would have more birthdays and that he and Great-grandpa Gail were going to sing her the birthday song from Heaven every time; and that it was too bad she had missed the party because he was sure she would have loved the strawberry shortcake. He asked if ZeZe knew about the garden and the animals in it, and he wondered if she would like their names or want to name them herself. He asked who took care of the animals for ZeZe; and then the *BIG* question.

"When will ZeZe get here?"

The grandparents told Bradey that they knew his Grandma ZeZe when she was as little as him; and that her name was 'Becca' and they sang lots of birthday songs to her while she was growing up on earth as their grand daughter. Grandma said it was okay that she missed the cake this once, because God had planted a Shortcake Tree along the fence of ZeZe's garden where she could someday nibble on her favorite dessert whenever she wanted to. She showed it to Bradey because it was on the border between her garden and ZeZe's so they could share it; and she pointed out the Strawberry Patch that was planted right beside it and the Whipped Cream cloud that rested on a silver pedestal close by. She told Bradey that Becca had always loved her grandma's garden and that they had both hoped that they would have gardens next door to each other in Heaven. Then she said the animals would probably be a nice surprise, but the peacocks were named after two of ZeZe's favorite colors—turquoise and coral—so she thought she would like them.

Grandpa told Bradey that the tigers, Ebony and Alabaster, were named by ZeZe in a story she wrote one time about Heaven; but that she probably didn't know they would *really be here* waiting for her when she arrived! He said the animals could take care of themselves in Heaven, and that ZeZe would probably be very happy about that; but that she would like the heavenly animals so much more than the earthly ones because they weren't dirty and they didn't stink, so he didn't think she would "care a whit" even if they did need a little care now and then. He also told him that sometimes "grandsons" did those kinds of things for their grandmothers, and that he thought one of The Brothers was going to get the job of caring for ZeZe's animals some day.

THE LITTLEST WARRIOR

About the *BIG* question, Grandma Hazel explained that only God knows when people should be called away to Heaven; that ZeZe would come as soon as it was her turn to leave Earth, and that she knew ZeZe would be delighted if Bradey would stop in now and then and check on the animals.

Then she added with a wink, "And besides, I need a little boy to come over and eat my cookies and play in my fountain and sit in my swing!" And of course Bradey Josheb was delighted to have the honor of accommodating the Double-great Grandmother in these important tasks.

Bradey had learned so much while visiting Grandma Hazel's garden that his cherubic brain was spinning; but there was one more thing she wanted to show him. Not far from the fountain was a pretty little tree with some purplish "bulbs" hanging on it. Grandpa Doc lifted Bradey onto the lowest branch and told him to climb around and pick some of those "figs". While he was picking, and putting them into a little basket, Grandma Hazel told a story of when ZeZe was a little girl in Redlands, California. She said that she had a fig tree in her back yard and when the grandchildren came over to visit she would pick fresh figs and cut them up, putting them in bowls with cream and sugar. She explained further.

"Becca loved them soooo much that she would have eaten them until they made her sick if I hadn't told her she'd had enough! I want you to taste them, too, Bradey!"

So they walked back through the garden toward the cottage and before they got there the sound of beautiful piano music met their ears.

"What's that?" Bradey queried.

"Oh, it must be Bernice!" Grandma smiled. "She's your great aunt, Grandpa Gail's sister. She comes over to visit me and plays my piano for me. Isn't it beautiful! Wait 'til you see it! But let's walk yer grandpa to the gate; he's going over to spend some time with the boys."

Grandpa Doc looked puzzled and reached for another cookie, for grandma had retrieved the plate from the garden table and brought it to the cottage. "Where are you sendin' me now, Hazel?" he queried.

"I'm not sendin' you anyplace, Doc. You said the boys were waitin' for you over at Wayne's place; I guess the cookies made you forget. Here, let me fill a basket with them and you can take it with you. Since Bernice is here, I imagine Kenneth and Dale are with the other fellas." And she scurried inside to get more cookies for Grandpa Doc to take with him.

Grandpa wandered to the gate to pat his horse's neck and Bradey followed him, swinging his fig basket. He let the bunny loose and took a plump fig in his hand, reaching as high as he could toward the horse's nose.

"What's his name, Grandpa? Does he like figs?"

"You bet he does!" Grandpa nodded, lifting Bradey to sit on the fence. "Hold out yer hand and he'll gobble it right up!" which he did, making Bradey laugh and shiver at the same time.

"Yessirree, Bradey-boy!" Grandpa chuckled. "Ol' Trail Boss will do about anything for one of yer

Gran'mama's fresh figs. Tell 'im to '*circle*' an' see what he does."

"Circle, Tray-boss!" Bradey shouted, and giggled with excitement when the majestic animal obeyed by keeping his back feet in place and prancing in a circle several times.

"He-heeeee!" Grandpa laughed as Bradey fetched another fig from the basket and fed it to Trail Boss. "Ain't that somethin', Bradey? He's a fine animal, that's fer sure!" and he patted the horse's neck and rubbed his nose.

Grandma Hazel was bustling across the lawn now and handed the basket of cookies to Grandpa, who swung up onto Trail Boss's back. Bradey wanted to go with him, and he knew it so he hollered, as he trotted down the Golden Road.

"You eat up all them figs, now, an' keep yer Gran'mamma happy, an' next time you can go with me an' the boys!" With a tip of his hat, Greater-grandpa Doc was galloping down the road on his fine horse with Bradey gazing after him.

Inside the cottage Bradey's wide, brown eyes darted from here to there, taking in all the fascination of the double-great grandmother's abode. She had sat him down on a puffy, red couch to listen to Aunt Bernice's piano playing while she went in the kitchen to prepare the fresh figs and cream; but at first he took in all the sites. There were lacey doilies on shiny tables with crystal bowls of smooth, mouth-watering fruit; a tidy book case; a very intriguing rocking chair with fluffy pillows; and a delicate little hutch full of interesting treasures.

Bradey was awestruck to see the colors of music drifting about the room; for with every note that Great-aunt Bernice played came beautiful and innumerable colors and scents, thrilling the cherub's senses in a mesmerizing utopia. The piano was white with gold trim—sort of like an earthly Baby Grand—and she let him peek under the propped lid and watch the little hammers tap out melodies on the piano wires inside. She taught him some little songs with motions; like *Climb Up Sonshine Mountain,* and *I'm Happy All the Time.* Bradey laughed and cavorted about, deciding that he loved music and dancing and singing! Then he wanted to play the piano so Great-aunt Bernice lifted him up onto the silky, gold-tasseled bench beside her and let him finger the ivory keys to the tune of *Jesus Loves the Little Children.*

Soon Grandma Hazel called them to the table where they all enjoyed the refreshment she had prepared. Bradey didn't know about cream, so Grandma took great delight in explaining all about cows, and how she used to have to "milk" them on earth and wait for the cream to rise to the top, and then make her own butter by shaking it until it curdled. Bradey was completely intrigued by her stories about life on earth, and about people in Bradey's family and he could have listened for a long time; but Grandma Hazel said she had a surprise for him, and told him to reach into his Miracle Pocket for the next gift.

Bradey drew out the little nickel and copper garden spade and studied it with great curiosity. Grandma was already off on the next adventure and Bradey had to trot to keep up with her as she left the cottage and headed for another corner of her garden, talking all the way about "seeds" and "growing things". Just behind the cottage she showed him a patch of bare ground. She told Bradey all about God creating the earth from nothing and how he planted a garden in Eden. As she showed him how to dig with his little spade and plant seeds in the ground, she told him about the Fall of Man and how hard it was to grow things after that because of "weeds" and "pests" and things. As they walked to the fountain to fill a little watering can, she explained how God made things to grow when they are fed, watered and cared for...and how it works for plants, animals and even children; but that it's much better in Heaven because there are no weeds or diseases and everything turns out perfect.

Bradey's little head was spinning with new input as he sprinkled the Living Water on his newly planted seeds and crawled up into double-great grandmother's lap to hear about "farmers" on earth and how hard they worked for their "harvest"; about storms and drought and floods; and finally about all God's "blessings" for getting through "life" and the "rewards" that wait for his children in Heaven when their earthly journey is over. By the time she finished the story, little green stems were popping up from Bradey's garden and he watched with fascination as they grew into a row of snapdragons right before his eyes! Grandma showed him how to pick a blossom and squeeze it a certain way to make it "talk" and Bradey giggled with delight.

Basking in the Light of the Lamb in Grandma Hazel's garden Bradey was perfectly content, thinking about all the wonderful things he had seen and learned and all the relatives and friends he had met, when they heard singing and music from the park across the road. Bradey craned his little neck for a closer look but there were too many bushes in the way. So Grandma said she would take him there.

"It's probably your Great-great Grandpa LaVern," she speculated. "He likes to meet in the park with the great Evangelists and talk about revival on Earth and the Great Battle between good and evil."

Grandma showed him how to open the lid of the garden bench where he could stow his spade and watering can.

"You can come and plant seeds in your garden any time you want," she smiled. "All over Heaven you will see beautiful things growing, and you can gather the seeds and bring them here to plant if you want to!"

Bradey grinned, remembering all those Goodie Bushes in Kids' Paradise, and wondered if he could grow one by planting a gumdrop.

Outside the gate, they crossed the Golden Road into the park. Some parrots perched on the trees nearby; and a big, fluffy cat with silvery fur and white paws sunned itself on a smooth rock, flicking its large, white-tipped tail and purring loudly. Bradey stopped to look at it, and noticed its green and yellow eyes and long whiskers. The cat stretched and sprang from the rock to the grassy path, following Bradey toward the group of men in the park. Grandpa LaVern looked up and smiled broadly. He squatted down to greet Bradey with a hug, ruffling his hair and pinching his cherry-blossom cheek. Then he reached out for a handshake and spoke to Grandma Hazel.

"Praise the Lord, Sister Bryan!" and she answered.

"I'm glad to see you, Brother Mussell! Bradey and I heard the music and thought you might be nearby!"

THE LITTLEST WARRIOR

"Oh, yes!" he exclaimed. "It's a Worship Cluster of young people."

He pointed to a big circle of white sand surrounded by huge trees with white bark and bright, spring-green leaves on wide-spread branches that left plenty of room for the Light of the Lamb to shine through onto the area below. Many rambling Wisteria grew among the trees and the vines had crawled to the treetops, filling their branches with gorgeous lavender and white blossoms that hung in dainty clusters three to five feet long! In the Circle of Crystal Sand stood a pearly gazebo; silver benches with deep purple cushions were scattered all around so people could sit and watch the goings on. Today, the "goings on" was a group of young women dressed in flowing, silky garments of all colors that reminded Bradey of the rainbow he had seen on Mount Witness. Their movements were as fluid as a smooth river as they danced and sang their praises to the Most High.

"We were listening to some of our grand-daughters while we talked about God's great Plan of the Ages," Grandpa LaVern smiled again.

He took Bradey by the hand and introduced him to some of his friends, D.L. Moody, John Wycliff, and Hudson Taylor. Then the Evangelists wandered toward the Circle of Crystal Sand to listen to the singing. So, Grandma Hazel told Bradey, with a hug and a kiss, that she would see him later and she walked back across the road to her cottage.

Great-great Grandpa LaVern sat down on a park bench and the furry cat jumped into his lap. He petted its fur and reached into his pocket.

"See this?" he said to Bradey, holding a thin, shiny gadget in the palm of his hand—like one of those earthly compact mirrors that women carried in their purses. "Reach into your Miracle Pocket and you will find my gift to you." Bradey obeyed and drew out a small, golden disc.

"It's a Praise Wheel." He smiled. "When I was on Earth, I used a tape recorder to save the voices of my grand children; and that one, "he gestured, pointing to Bradey's, " is *your mama* singing a song when she wasn't much bigger than you!"

Then he opened his streamlined, heavenly disc-player and allowed Bradey to put his little Praise Wheel inside. Immediately, the disc began to turn, emitting small flames of color and a very pleasant scent into the air as a tiny, sweet voice began to sing, *"This is the day that the Lord has made; Not like tomorrow or yesterday; He made today in a special way; So let's all sing and be glad..."* Bradey loved it, but was more fascinated by the fact that this tiny voice was his mother's than by the gadgets that had preserved her praise.

Great-great Grandpa LaVern played other discs for Bradey, of other children he had recorded singing God's praises on Earth; he explained that praise to the Most High is never lost or forgotten, because God loves the praises of His people. Then he told Bradey about the library vault at The Great Hall of Music where he could find hundreds of thousands of praise recordings. Then he explained that he likes to play his all the time, so The Master had given him his own special player to carry around Heaven; but that there were *Praise Pedestals* scattered about Heaven in all the parks and resting places where people could listen to their favorite Praise Wheels.

THE LITTLEST WARRIOR

"There's one right over here," he pointed to a mini-garden at the edge of the park near the Golden Road where a comfy garden swing like Grandma Hazel's sat next to a butterfly bush with red-violet blooms. The bush was covered with multi-colored butterflies of all sizes and a golden pedestal stood nearby. Bradey ran ahead to try his Praise Wheel on the Praise Pedestal and was swinging happily on the garden swing enjoying his music before Grandpa and the cat caught up with him.

"Grandpa 'Vern," Bradey questioned. "Are there more Praise Wheels of my mom in the library?"

"Oh, yes!" Grandpa answered, patting Bradey's back, "and I'm going to take you there. But would you like to go watch the dancing for awhile first? Sarah's over there."

"She is?" Bradey's brown eyes brightened, remembering his tall, graceful cousin who welcomed him so sweetly at his Grand Reception, and whose sweet voice of song ushered the King of Kings into Celebration Hall.

"Yes, let's!" he chirped happily. He wanted to run ahead again all the way to the pearly gazebo, but on second thought, decided to walk with his grandfather and the cat.

Slipping his chubby, dimpled hand into Grandpa LaVern's very large one, he asked, "Is this your cat?"

"Yes," said the grandfather, scruffing the kitty's fur once more before heading toward the Circle of Crystal Sand. "This is Fluff. Almost everywhere I go, he seems to follow."

Arriving at the edge of the circle, Great-great Grandpa picked out a spot on one of the purple-cushioned silver benches and sat down with Fluff, pointing out Sarah to Bradey, as she skipped and danced, swirling her silky scarves to the music. She caught a glimpse of them as they entered the circle, and immediately skipped off the platform and across the soft sand in her bare feet to greet them.

Bradey thought she looked like an angel as she wrapped him in a silky hug and said, "Hi, Bradey! Hi Grandpa! I'm so glad to see you both! We are having such a wonderful time singing and dancing our praises to the Most High! I have found so many friends who love to sing and dance like me, so we have decided to adopt the name of *Celestial Rainbows* and to travel all over Heaven singing and dancing in every gazebo we can find to share our songs of praise with everyone!"

"That's wonderful, Sarah! You were born to praise the Lord, and all The Redeemed of Heaven will share in your worship as you sing and dance," Grandpa LaVern said.

Then she ran back to the gazebo, bubbling over with joy, to sing and dance to her heart's content. After watching for awhile, Bradey and Grandpa LaVern decided to go to the Music Library. They had a wonderful walk down the Golden Road as Grandpa pointed out lots of interesting things to Bradey. Soon one of Grandpa's evangelist friends rode up in a beautifully engraved cart pulled by a black and auburn horse. He gave them a ride to the library and dropped them off at the gate.

THE LITTLEST WARRIOR

Inside the Great Hall of Music there were many rooms with large stages. Each stage was decorated with the riches of a different culture and different types of music were being played on each platform. The rooms were like theaters, where people could come and see the offerings of praise to the Most High by gifted musicians from every tribe and people. Bradey was fascinated by the varied instruments and unique clothing of different cultures, and it took some time—which, of course, is not a problem in Heaven—to see the sights.

Finally, they found their way to the Music Library. Bradey was surprised to see that it was a large space, but smaller than the theaters, with a vaulted ceiling that was open at the top to let the Light of the Lamb flood the room. Angels of Music were busy about the room, finding Praise Wheels for people who had come to the library to check out special music. Grandpa LaVern talked to one of the angels who took them to a special wall of golden drawers. One drawer was engraved, *Angela Cheri Howell-Markis*; it was a small drawer, just big enough for a small stack of music wheels, yet whenever one was lifted there was always another underneath. All the songs that Bradey's mother had ever sung to the Lord were in this little golden drawer, and Bradey felt very warm and comforted inside to know that he could come to this place and hear his mother's voice again and again. The Angel of Music explained to Bradey that he could come whenever he wanted and play his mom's Praise Wheels at the library; or take some with him on a heavenly adventure so he could play them on Praise Pedestals wherever he was going; or *even* take them to one of the theaters here in the Hall of Music and request the musicians onstage to play his mother's praise in their unique fashion, performing it with their own cultural instruments. It was like a dream that would never end, and Bradey left the Great Hall of Music with his little cherub head reeling, full of ideas and adventures.

Outside, on the wide marble steps, Grandpa LaVern and Bradey were distracted by a commotion on the Golden Road below. As they descended the steps and neared the excited crowd, they saw that Sarah was among them.

"Sarah!" Bradey called. "What's everybody so excited about?"

"Oh, Bradey!" she said breathlessly, running to them, "Come with me! Someone else is coming Home! The Grand Reception is being planned and my *Celestial Rainbows* get to dance and sing at the celebration!"

"Who's coming, Sarah?" Bradey wondered, wide-eyed.

"I'm not sure," Sarah said, taking his hand. "I think it's another double-great grandmother."

Grandpa LaVern smiled broadly and thought fondly of his own dear Addie who would soon be passing her 100th birthday on Earth; then he added with a twinkle in his eye, "In that case, perhaps I should come with you."

Bradey had gone back to the Royal Corrals at Champion Ranch with Great-grandpa Gail after the Welcome Home Celebration; which was not for Addie, as some supposed, but for yet *another* Great-grandmother named Jo (which is *entirely* another story!)

Meanwhile, back at the ranch, they went into the Heavenly Tack Barn and got their duds on. Bradey was exceptionally proud of his black cowboy hat and black and gold cowboy boots! He loved his chaps and his silky fringed white shirt; and, of course, his tiny black Levis with bright copper stitching and the golden *"CR"* embroidered on the pocket. He decided right away that, if the Master had not already made him a Warrior, he might like to be a Cowboy!

Coming out of the barn, Bradey stepped into the warm, sweet Light of the Lamb and flashed a dimpled smile upwards in cherubic appreciation for this common comfort of Heaven, with absolutely no recollection that this perfect light replaced the scorching sun of the earth below. Bradey saw that Reece Ryder was busy working Prince Kye in the middle of the main corral and, glancing sideways, he noticed that the stable boys, Toby Jasper and Tate Marshall, were leading Champion across the grass toward him.

"Hey, mates!" he hollered to them, hopping up on the fence to get a closer look. "Where ya been?"

"We been ridin'!" Toby grinned, pearly teeth shining. "Up da mountain an' back agin!"

"Awesome!" Bradey answered. "Whatcha doin' now?"

"Hey, Bradey!" Tate waved. "We're brushin' 'im now. He's gotta get a drink of Living Water and cool down a bit. The Master's comin' to take 'im for another ride soon."

"He is?" Bradey was thrilled at the thought. "Where's he goin' this time?" The boys both grinned from ear to ear, just as Great-grandpa Gail stepped up and pushed Bradey's hat down onto his little pug nose.

"Don't know fer sure, grandson; but you better get out there and work your pony so you can be done by the time King Jesus gets here. You're goin' with Him!"

Bradey shivered with excitement! "I am? AWESOME!!" he shouted, thrusting a dimpled fist into the air and jumping to the ground from the fence rail.

He headed for Cherub's stall, glancing inconspicuously behind him at the poof of gold dust that hung in a tiny cloud just above the ground where his little boots had landed, and felt very pleased at his accomplishment. Grandpa Gail chuckled and helped Bradey get his lead rope and take Cherub into the ring. He taught him how to click his tongue to make Cherub go, how to flick the rope and command, "Git up!" to make him trot and how to wave his hat and holler, "Heyaw!" to get him to gallop in a circle. Then he taught him how to give the rope a little jerk and shout, "Walk!" to slow him down again, and then, "Whoa!" and "Easy, boy" to stop him and make him stand still and watch while Bradey walked up to him and gave him some good, strong pats on the neck. They were making wonderful progress and Bradey was proving himself to be quite the little cowboy, to his grandfather's delight; and, of course, Cherub was a regular saint because in Heaven all the animals love their people and obedience comes naturally, making the training "as easy as apple pie" (which Bradey didn't quite understand but had heard his grandpa say).

Reece had already put up Prince Kye with a delectable feed bag at his nose and was sitting atop the corral with a straw in his mouth, grinning. Toby and Tate had set up their brushing station as close to the stable door as possible so they could watch, too. All of them were thoroughly enjoying the tiny cowboy, all dressed in his ranch duds, learning his moves and commanding his little colt like a real trainer.

"O.K., Cowboy!" Grandpa ordered next. "Turn 'im loose and gimme yer rope," which Bradey did, fumbling a bit with the big clip on Cherub's harness.

"Now, git up on that bale of heavenly alfalfa and call 'im over to ya," he continued. "Just stand there 'til he comes; then grab a handful of mane and throw yer leg over 'is back."

"O.K. Grampa!" Bradey answered breathlessly, eyes wide with adventure. He ran as fast as his short legs could carry him in chaps and boots and clambered up onto the big bale. Grandpa Gail held Cherub fast by the halter and spoke softly in his ear.

"Watch 'im, now."

"Come, Cherub!" Bradey called and tried the whistling thing again, emitting a shrill sound that almost toppled him off his own feet. All the cowboys guffawed at the sight of Bradey startling himself with his own whistle.

"I did it, Ryder!" He squealed gleefully, with a wave to his friends at the edge of the corral. Toby and Tate had come out to watch the final episode and stood laughing and shouting encouragement along with Reece. Cherub, meanwhile, had tossed his little head at Bradey's whistle as if he was quite startled himself; but now he stood still beside Great-grandpa Gail. Grandpa let go of the harness, and swatted him gently on his furry rump.

"Git!" he encouraged the colt. "That little tyke's yer master now…go on!

Bradey was slapping both knees and calling him to come; he giggled delightedly as the little horse trotted obediently to his side and stood still while Bradey labored to get on his back. Then the shouting began. The young cowboys and ranch hands gathered 'round to watch the show as the little cowboy took another turn at "staying in the saddle", so to speak. Bradey rode Cherub around the corral a few times without incident while onlookers shouted their enthusiastic encouragement. Then Ryder opened the back gate and Cherub saw his chance to head for wide open spaces.

"Hang on, Mate!" ornery Ryder laughed as the little horse skittered through the opening. Bradey did very well staying on. Reece had leaped from the gate post onto Prince Kye's back, giving the feed bag a quick jerk and letting it fall to the ground.

"'Nuff fer now," he told his horse and, guiding him quickly through the gate, he trotted behind Bradey and

Cherub to the meadow, shouting instructions all the way.

"Lean forward!" he called when they went up a hill; and "Pull back a bit!" as they came back down; or "Rein 'im in, Matey!" if Cherub tried to run.

Soon the little ones were tired, however, and Cherub stumbled while coming around a little knoll and sloshed Bradey sideways just enough to dump him off into the cushy, cool meadow grass. Bradey rolled around, trying to get his feet under him, surprised that he was not hearing Ryder's laughter nearby; but as he pushed his hat up so he could see again, he was startled by some very large hooves only a few feet away from him, prancing gently and carefully about the little boy. Before Bradey could look up, strong hands around his torso lifted him from the grass, higher and higher, until suddenly he was looking into the smiling face of none other than the King of Heaven, Jesus the Master of All.

"So, my Littlest Warrior is a cowboy today!" he said with twinkling eyes and a firm but gentle hug.

Over The Master's shoulder, Bradey saw Ryder and Prince Kye, heading back through the corral gate leading Cherub by his rope. Jesus jostled him in his great arms then so he could look at his rosy face. Bradey's ears were very red and his breathing was short, kind of like the humming bird in Grandma Hazel's garden; but he managed a dimpled smile and a chirpy, "Yep!" as Jesus placed him on Champion's back and then mounted the stallion behind Bradey.

"We are going for another ride today," the Master informed him. "I have some things to tell you about."

THE LITTLEST WARRIOR

Champion stopped his prancing and walked slowly through the gate into the Royal Corrals. King Jesus stopped to tousle the hair of his stable boys, Toby and Tate, saying, "Thanks, boys. I'll be back soon and he'll need another good brushing."

"Yes, Master," the boys answered together, wearing proud smiles under the modest gaze they had respectfully given the King.

Even Jesus chuckled as Bradey waved and said, "Later, Gators!" to his friends.

The King was reaching down now to shake Great-grandpa Gail's hand. Grandpa took Bradey from Champion's back and walked him into the tack barn to take off all his duds and hang them up in his special place. Bradey sat down on his little bench to pull off his boots and spoke with a sigh of relief.

"I love my duds, Grandpa; but it sure feels good to wiggle my toes again! They like to breathe."

Grandpa threw his head back and laughed out loud, and then, hanging up Bradey's hat he said in a low voice, "Well, sir, I see your point; but for an old cowboy, there's nothin' like a good pair o' boots!"

Bradey buckled his tiny belt around his chubby belly and checked his small sheath for his orange rose; yes, it was safe and sound. Thrusting a dimpled hand into the treat bag hanging nearby, he ran over to Cherub's stall and patted his fuzzy nose. Then he flattened his hand and let the pony find the Golden Nibbles, which were gobbled with a gleeful snort.

"Good job, Cherub!" Bradey complimented, patting his nose again. "You were almost as good as Champion out there!"

"You betcha!" Grandpa chuckled. "Like father, like son…he'll be a beauty; that's for sure!"

Then Bradey's pink toes flew skyward as Grandpa swung him nearly upside down and hoisted him onto his shoulders, then snapped at his feet as if to eat them as Bradey squealed with childish delight. Approaching The King of Heaven once again, Grandpa handed the happy cherub up to the Master and Bradey settled his little bottom comfortably onto the cushy, velvet coverlet on Champion's broad back.

"Well, done, Gail Bryan," he heard the Master say to Grandpa, adding sincerely. "You are a faithful steward of the Royal Corrals. I am pleased with the colt and the training of my horses. You have shown great skill with my young ranch hands as well…and with your grandson!" He patted Bradey's back.

Grandpa Gail looked up at the King and answered gratefully and with utmost respect, "Yes, my Lord. I am grateful for the opportunity to serve."

"Go, Champion…" the Master sat up tall on his great steed and looked out across his Heaven. "Go to The Chronicles of Time and Eternity."

Bradey leaned back now, enveloping himself in the folds of the King's vesture. He was remembering his first ride and preparing for the thrills of another. This ride was not so stunning as the first, however; King Jesus did not seem to be in a hurry to get to The Chronicles. Champion held his head high and stepped purposefully, prancing sideways from time to time, but did not run; or fly. King Jesus pointed out many interesting things along the Golden Road and Bradey asked questions about almost all of them. They saw many and varied types of Heaven's plant and animal life; and everything they passed acknowledged the King of Heaven in its own special way.

Soon the Golden Road took a slight turn and wound upwards through a cluster of heather hills until—at the top of the highest one—they came to a sort of amphitheater. There was a semicircular gallery of seats arranged in tiers; but instead of facing a stage they faced the edge of the hill that dropped down into a deep ravine. So there was nothing to be seen from a sitting position except the blues skies of Heaven. Surrounding the gallery of seats were large marble pillars with engraved inscriptions that said things like:

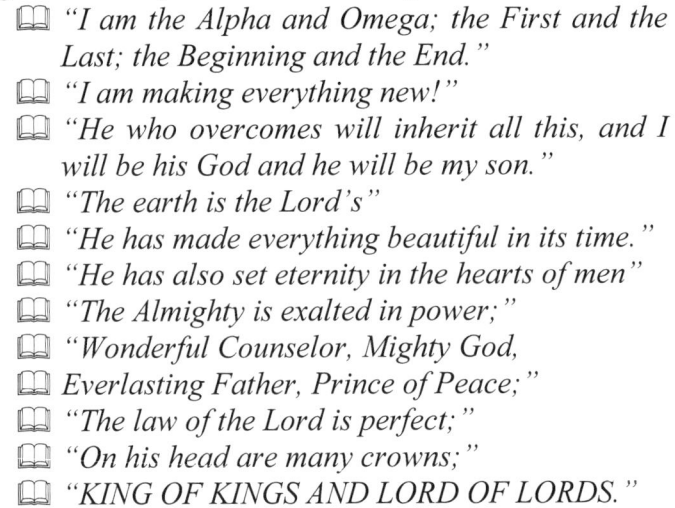

- *"I am the Alpha and Omega; the First and the Last; the Beginning and the End."*
- *"I am making everything new!"*
- *"He who overcomes will inherit all this, and I will be his God and he will be my son."*
- *"The earth is the Lord's"*
- *"He has made everything beautiful in its time."*
- *"He has also set eternity in the hearts of men"*
- *"The Almighty is exalted in power;"*
- *"Wonderful Counselor, Mighty God, Everlasting Father, Prince of Peace;"*
- *"The law of the Lord is perfect;"*
- *"On his head are many crowns;"*
- *"KING OF KINGS AND LORD OF LORDS."*

Above the gallery, built into the structure of marble pillars was a special open room. It was like the special Opera Seats in the old theaters that were reserved for royalty or VIPs; except it was larger. A marble staircase wound upwards on each side of the room, ending at arched doorways that were secured by regal angelic guardians. In the center was a marble seat veined with gold. Two giant diamonds cut like the rounded end of a king's scepter sat on the posts of its back. The arms were draped with red velvet coverlets with golden tassels on the corners; red velvet cushions padded the seat and back of the huge chair. Exquisite flowering trees stood in golden pots behind the central throne on either side, and a coffered ceiling emitted a bright amber glow along the back wall that made the marble throne and its occupant appear shrouded like silhouettes before a setting sun.

Bradey was so enraptured by the King's extraordinary chamber that he did not notice the affectionate pleasure on the face of The Master that turned the corners of His mouth into a grin and made His deep, loving eyes twinkle merrily. He sat down on His marble throne and watched with amusement as Bradey's brown eyes widened with each new discovery; and the little gasps that escaped his cherry-cherub lips from time to time were more enjoyable still.

Turning slowly in circles, Bradey saw that the side walls of The Master's chamber were black velvet, studded with diamonds that looked just like the night lights in the Master's universe. Bradey's eyes brightened as he reached for a big purple grape on a cluster that hung delectably over the edge of a shining crystal dish on the small marble table beside the throne; and only then did he notice the large snow leopard lying in the corner with emerald-green eyes and a very pink tongue! He was startled at first; and then drew in a slow, "Ahhh!" as he focused on the dimly-lit corner and saw that there were two. The big one was slightly in front of the other, and they were purring contently.

THE LITTLEST WARRIOR

Curiosity immediately prevailed over Bradey's initial shock and he glanced sideways at the King with a shy dimpled grin and questioning eyebrows.

"Can I touch him?" he asked timidly.

Jesus answered with a wave of his hand and a father's delight.

"Of course you can touch him. You can even sit on him if you want to. His name is Raj."

Bradey squatted before the majestic beast and gently scratched between his ears, fascinated by the silvery fur with black spots. Then the King spoke in a commanding voice.

"Charú, bring your gift."

From the shadows behind Raj the female leopard arose quickly and came forward with a squirming ball of fur in her mouth, setting it down gently in front of Bradey. Bradey was too overcome with delight to speak at first; but as the leopard cub began to mew he burst with excitement.

"A baby one! Is he mine? I love him!" Then picking him up and holding him to his cheek, Bradey asked, "He feels soft, like a whispering wind. Does he have a name? Can he ride with me on Champion?"

"Yes, yes, yes!" King Jesus chuckled. "He is yours; his name is Jangi *[Jongee]* and it means *warrior*; but since he is still so small, you may call him *Whisper* if you wish. Now climb up into my chair with him and look out into the great blue expanse of my universe. It is time for you to learn about the world that you came from; the story of planet Earth."

Soon Bradey was snuggled comfortably on the very large and hospitable lap of The Master and Whisper was curled up on the very small but friendly lap of the Littlest Warrior; and the heavenly kitten was asleep and purring softly before the first scene of the story began to roll.

The blue skies of Heaven in front of the gallery turned black as coal, and The Chronicles of Time and Eternity began to unravel before Bradey's awestruck eyes. A tiny speck of golden light far, far away began to grow; moving closer and closer until it took the form of a glorious throng of angels singing the music of heaven as King Jesus began to narrate the story before them.

"There was a time when all of the angels of the Heavenly Realm were content to worship before the Father's throne continually and to do all His bidding, as they should. They were beautiful creatures, formed by the hand of Him who created all things for His glory..."

The company of angels sang a superlative anthem of praise and Bradey was particularly taken with the leader of the band, a magnificent angel—much larger than the rest—whose voice was a choir in itself. He led the others with powerful skill, drawing their voices together like a rushing river of musical resonance that filled the atmosphere with abundant energy and great joy.

"But then Lucifer became proud, believing that he could be like God if he wanted to; and he became dissatisfied with his commission. Now pride is an evil spirit that does not belong in the Kingdom of God; so it began immediately to corrupt God's creatures and enable Lucifer to lead them astray. But God would not share his glory with another; and Lucifer was punished for his rebellion. God took away his glory and cast him out of heaven with all the angels who had foolishly believed his lies;" and with a loud crash of thunder and a blinding flash of light that made Bradey flinch, he watched a ball of fire burn across the dark expanse and fall, and fall, and fall into oblivion. Then a silver whirlwind began to stir in the darkness as Jesus continued...

"Now, in the beginning, God had created the Earth; because there was nothing there until He created it. Out of the darkness he said, *Let there be light*."

Bradey watched the scenes with fascination as the planet Earth appeared and began to spin in the atmosphere, surrounded by stars and planets, sun and moon. He was glued to the "screen" as Jesus described the separating of ocean and sky, the growth of plants and trees and the creation of the animal kingdom, the birds of the air and the fish of the sea.

"On the sixth day of Creation," Jesus continued, "God made man—a creature formed in his own likeness—to bring him pleasure and to rule over the rest of his creation. Then he made a wife for the man, and he named them Adam and Eve; and told them to fill his earth and take care of it for him. God was very pleased with his earth and his people and he called his creation *very good*. But, remember, Lucifer had been cast out of heaven; and he was very angry at God. So when he saw God's new creation, he decided to see if he could destroy it; and to get God's people to follow <u>him</u> instead of God."

Bradey sat up tall on Jesus' lap, nearly jostling Whisper onto the floor, as he watched the account of The Fall. He was astonished to see that Eve was so easily convinced that God's words were not really true; and that Adam so easily slipped into her delusion. He was horrified, placing both chubby palms on the sides of his face, when God banished his people from the Garden of Eden and told them that since they had disobeyed his commands, they would struggle for life until the day of their death.

"The world became a wicked place, then," Jesus said, "because God's people had relinquished their stewardship to Lucifer, God's enemy, who is called Satan. He blinded the eyes of all humanity to the truth so that they did not listen to God at all, but did evil things continually that caused the Father to grieve over the world he had made. He wanted to destroy it; but there was one man on the earth who still loved God and served him. His name was Noah."

Bradey could hardly contain himself as he watched the account of The Great Deluge, his tiny, little heart pitter-pattering with anticipation; and when the flood was over and the rainbow appeared, Bradey clapped his dimpled hands. King Jesus explained the meaning of the rainbow and when Bradey realized how important it was he knew why he had wanted so badly to send one to his mother that first day. He reminded Jesus of his request and the Lord smiled with sovereign intent and answered him gently.

"Yes, I remember; and a very special delivery will soon be sent to Earth with your mother's name on it. This little rainbow will also be a promise of life and will represent God's favor on your earthly family; I know you will be very pleased."

THE LITTLEST WARRIOR

Although the Story of the World would have taken days and weeks to watch on earthly movie screens, it was only minutes in Heaven before Jesus was talking about God's remedy for fallen mankind.

"Remember the story I told you on your first day in Heaven, Bradey Josheb? About how I went to Earth to fulfill the Father's plan of salvation?"

A sizeable shiver went down Bradey's cherubic spine as the vivid scenes on God's universal display recalled the accounts of Jesus' birth, ministry, death and resurrection. Once again Bradey shouted with elation.

"You won!" as the empty tomb told the world that Jesus was the Son of God.

Nevertheless, as we earthlings well know, the story continued in the valley of struggle; and Jesus had to explain to Bradey about the current war with evil on Earth. Both realms of Earth and Heaven now burst upon the scene as the Lord described how Heaven's witnesses watch the epic journey of the saints, and why the angels rush to their assistance in their fierce battle against the Enemy of their souls. That small but brilliant light of eternal intelligence began to gleam in Bradey's mind then, as he understood that this history of the world completely explained the current preparations going on in Heaven.

They sat quietly for a time; it was like an intermission at an old movie. Even for a heavenly mind, it seemed like a lot to process; and taking one of the King's very large, smooth hands in both of his little ones, Bradey crinkled his eyebrows and looked a long time at the ugly scar in the center of his Master's palm.

Finally, he looked up at Jesus' face with both sorrow and resolve and said—very solemnly for such a little tyke—"King Jesus, we still need to win some more, don't we?"

Wrapping the cherub in his arms of love and peace, Jesus answered strongly, "Yes, we do; but the Father's plan has no holes in it. Even now we are preparing for the Final Battle in which you will some day fight. For you have been gifted as a Holy Warrior and will be trained to ride with Me to victory."

Without looking up, Bradey slowly posed another question to his Lord. "But, what about my dad…and The Brothers? Are they training for the Battle, too?"

With a note of sadness, King Jesus answered, standing Bradey up in front of him and looking straight into his eyes. "I want them to, but they do not see it as clearly as you do. I intercede earnestly for my people on Earth before my Father's throne because their lives are cluttered with the things of the world. To them, Life on Earth is large and loud; but the true battle is very faint and distant. Satan works continually to cloud their vision and separate them from their eternal destinies."

Suddenly, a great concern spread over Bradey's face as he asked, "But, do they not have a sword to fight him with?"

"Yes," Jesus replied, "They do have a sword, kept in a sheath on a bookshelf."

"But have you told them how to use it yet? Can't you tell them what to do?" Bradey continued with concern.

THE LITTLEST WARRIOR

With the greatest kindness and the most loving, patient gaze, the Lord of All looked out into the expanse of the heavens and answered.

"I speak to my people often, my Little Warrior; but earthly ears are dull, and do not quickly recognize my voice. Remember the thunder?"

Bradey, of course, had perfect trust, despite the dilemma facing his family and God's other people on Earth; and Jesus comforted him even more by reminding him of the angels that are constantly dispatched to fight for the saints. He also told him that God has gifted messengers on the earth to bring truth to them: evangelists, pastors, prophets and teachers.

"It is also important for you to know that your own mother is one of those messengers. Did you know that her name – Angela Cheri--means *messenger, chosen of God*?" Bradey brightened as his Lord continued. "She is a different kind of messenger, of the elite Order of Intercessors, who do battle on their knees in prayer. See her there? She prays for them now."

Bradey turned and looked below to see his mother on her knees in prayer. Through her tear-stained eyes, she saw an open book lying before her on the floor; but Bradey saw a gleaming sword that glistened with promise in the dim light of Earth's meager day. His little heart leaped within him as he heard the names of his dad and brothers lifted in prayer from her lips; and he watched with exhilaration as the gathering angels of the Heavenly Realm acted swiftly on her requests. It was a powerful ending to an amazing story. Bradey was still as darling a cherub as ever, but in his keen little accelerated mind, he almost felt like a man. So he was not surprised when the Master rose from His throne in the chamber and said these words.

"Now that you know the story of Earth's Epic Battle, it will soon be time for us to make a visit to Yashobam's camp."

Bradey sucked in his sweet breath as a sizeable shiver went down his angelic spine. He was very excited about going to Yashobam's camp. Jesus rose and took Bradey by the hand, scooping up Whisper with the other arm.

"You will love Camp Conquest when the time comes, my Little Warrior;" King Jesus said as they descended the staircase to the gallery below. "But right now we have a little errand to run; I have a special rainbow to deliver."

Bradey shot a glance far up to his Master's face, which was met with a wink and a nod. Bradey's excitement erupted into cherubic giggles, then; and he skipped down the stairs thinking aloud.

"Heaven is very full of great adventures! Toby was right when he said, *There ain't no better place for boys to be!*"

He ran the rest of the way to where Champion stood grazing peacefully, and startled him with a squeal of delight that made him toss his majestic head and snort.

" C'mon, Champion! Get ready to fly, cuz its time for my mama's rainbow!"

The Heavenly Kingdom was all astir as the Master and his cherub warrior wound back down the glittering trail on Champion's broad back through the heather hills that had led them to the amphitheater. Bradey was immediately occupied by the bustling and the chatter on the road below. Flowers were being gathered in big baskets, people were laughing and singing, and the birds and butterflies were flitting about like something wonderful was in the air; and, in fact, it was!

Bradey heard a group of women and girls talking excitedly together at the side of the road and one of them said "Have you heard about Bradey's Rainbow?"

"Yes!" chirped another merrily in return. "And today is the day! We must gather the softest ferns; and Baby's Breath; and lavender!"

"And pink and red roses!" someone added.

"And ladybugs!" said a chubby little girl with long brown locks dangling down her back.

Bradey was fascinated with their eager conversation, and wondered why they needed to gather any colors at all when a rainbow was so colorful already. Then he noticed cart after cart, coming from the direction of Sir Betters Bakery, loaded with the most delectable desserts. His mouth watered as they passed by and one of the jolly bakers tossed a heavenly marshmallow that landed with a plop in Bradey's lap.

THE LITTLEST WARRIOR

He popped it into his mouth without hesitation and asked with a full-cheeked grin, "King Jesus, where is everybody going?"

"The same place we are going, Bradey Josheb; to the Birthday Palace for the Rainbow Celebration! His wonderful smile was full of mystery and his deep, kind eyes twinkled with joy. Bradey looked around again at all the activity on the road and gave the classic shrug of a little boy who had no idea what was going on, but was just happy to be there.

Champion turned at a fork in the Golden Road that led towards Kids' Paradise. The happy noise of the children playing bounced back and forth onto Bradey's little ears like a flock of miniature super balls. Laughter, shouts, and cheers coming down the road brought back the wonder of that place from Bradey's first visit. He knew that the Birthday Palace was somewhere inside Kids' Paradise because Robert had pointed it out to him once before; but this would be his first time to see it inside.

Soon the festive peaks of the palace came into view and Bradey strained his chubby neck to see it more clearly. Bright colored flags flipped about in the breeze at the tops of the roof peaks and the Light of the Lamb softly lit the copper shingles on the palace turrets, making them shine like gold dust.

"I'm glad that we are having a celebration for my Rainbow; but how did all these people find out about it?" Bradey asked quizzically.

Jesus laughed heartily and answered, "Everybody loves a Special Delivery; and you will soon see why."

Jesus dismounted at the gate of Kids' Paradise and left Champion there to graze. He lifted Bradey down to the cool grass and put Whisper in the cherub's chunky arms. Soon Bradey was surrounded by happy children; they all wanted to see his new pet and ask questions about it. Bradey was so pleased to tell them all about getting Whisper that he almost forgot what they were there for. But King Jesus was in no hurry; he was watching his children with the greatest delight.

He walked over to the tree by the gate where Bradey had first met Reece Ryder and patted the slender tummy of a boy hanging upside down on a branch. Bradey had noticed the boy when they first arrived because he kept swinging from his knees and waving his arms. He thought the boy wanted to hold Whisper so he walked over and stretched his baby leopard toward the dangling child. But the boy only giggled as Whisper licked his very brown face with a scratchy tongue.

As Bradey turned back toward the crowd of children he heard Jesus say, "Ekundayo, how do you like my Heaven?"

"So very much, Master; especially the legs and arms," the boy answered, swinging off the limb to land on his feet before Jesus. The Master laughed at Dayo and squatted to embrace him.

"You were named well for, indeed, your *sorrow has become joy*! You are perfect from head to toe and I am so glad you are here with Me."

THE LITTLEST WARRIOR

Bradey looked at his own arms and legs in consternation, feeling sure that he had them from the start. This conversation between Jesus and Dayo, however, caused his cherub mind to wonder if some people get new ones when they arrive! A light punch on the shoulder interrupted his little boy thoughts.

"Hey, dude!" Robert said. "I'm glad you're back." Then he explained: "Ekundayo just got here. He told me all about his life on Earth. He's so cool! He lived in Niger, where nobody had enough food. His father was a peanut farmer—"

"What's a peanut?" Bradey quizzed his cousin.

"It's something you eat," Robert answered patiently. "They're round and crunchy and they pop out of a shell. Dayo's elephant, Jai—"

"What's an elephant?" Bradey interrupted again.

"You haven't seen an elephant yet? They're awesome! And huge! They kneel down so you can ride on their back. Dayo will show you his. Jai eats peanuts with the shells on. He loves them. I think one of your brothers loved peanuts—not with the shells!" he quickly clarified before Bradey could ask another question. "Anyway, Dayo was born with no arms and legs so he couldn't help his father on the peanut farm. One day his dad put him in a cart and told his mother to pull it down the road to the orphanage—"

"What's an orphanage?"

"Well, it's really sad, but it's a place for kids who don't have parents to take care of them. Anyway, Dayo was older than us—like twelve or something—and the orphanage wouldn't take him. So his mom was crying on the road and a Christian lady found them and gave them food. She told them all about Jesus and told Dayo's mother that she would take care of him. He lived with the lady for a little while but then he got real sick—"

"What does sick mean?"

"Sick is when a body stops working right; it only happens to earthly bodies. It makes them feel very bad and sometimes it makes them die. That's what happened to Dayo—he died from sickness and his Guardian brought him to Heaven. But since everything is perfect here, Dayo is a whole person now; he has arms and legs and he loves them so much he keeps using them to jump and climb and hang on trees!"

This made all the children laugh. Robert's stories always gathered a crowd. All at once, however, the whole group stared at Bradey and became wide-eyed with wonder. Bradey felt something fuzzy, wrinkled, and squirmy rub along his face and shoulder and then suddenly wrap around his waist! He looked up to see a gigantic gray animal with small eyes and big ears looking down at him from behind.

"Jai likes you!" called Dayo, running across the grass on his strong new legs and perfect feet.

The children laughed and squealed as Jai lifted Bradey Josheb high into the air and placed him squarely in the center of his back on a bright blue coverlet with silver trim and silver bells on the corners. Jai also wore a matching cap on the top of his head between his ears. It had a cluster of silver bells that hung down on his forehead and jingled merrily as he moved. Now Jai began to dance, stomping and swaying as only an elephant can, and Bradey screeched excitedly with every move.

"I'm as high as the trees!"

Then Jai stood still, for the Master moved toward him. He lowered his huge head and came down on one knee.

"Very good, Jai. You are a fine elephant!" King Jesus complimented. "Bradey and I have an engagement on the hill; but I am certain that someone in this group of beautiful children would love to have a ride on your back."

At this, the passel of kids began to jump and holler and wave their hands to get a ride on Jai's back. The Master lifted Bradey to the ground and took his hand. Together they began winding up the blossom-lined path to the top of the hill in the center of Kids' Paradise where the beautiful Birthday Palace gleamed over the landscape.

The stroll was exhilarating—even for a little tyke. The blossoming trees filled the air with their sweet perfume, and the melodious songs of innumerable feathered friends nestled in their branches mingled perfectly with the untold beauty in all directions.

"Dragonflies!" Bradey pointed. He was so pleased to know the names of things now that he was learning his way around.

"And hummingbirds!" He chimed out, his dark eyes dancing as he took in the sights and sounds.

Far away he saw the tops of edifices he had not yet visited and he remembered that Robert had promised to give him a grand tour of Kids' Paradise later. His little heart pattered with excitement to think of the many adventures that awaited him. Then a flutter caught his eye and he looked straight ahead. Bands of angels were moving busily about the palace going in and out. King Jesus saw Bradey's curiosity rising and smiled delightedly.

"The angels love these celebrations. The only thing more wonderful than a Special Delivery is a Homecoming!"

Coming closer and ascending the shallow steps to the great doorway, Bradey took a second look at those angels, recognizing some of them as the ones who had surrounded his mother when she was so sad; the ones God had sent when he heard Bradey's request. *What are they doing up here?* Bradey wondered. *I thought they were taking care of my mother.* He was not worried in the least, of course; because there is no worry in Heaven. But he was very curious and decided to ask The Master.

"King Jesus, why are the Ministering Angels at the Rainbow Celebration instead of taking care of my mom?"

Jesus laughed with great amusement and answered, "Many of them are with your mother even now; but these are here because this celebration is a very important part of taking care of her. They are going to deliver the Rainbow you requested!"

Before Bradey could ask any more questions, two guardians approached. One was Anchorr, whom

THE LITTLEST WARRIOR

Bradey Josheb was very glad to see and the other he did not know. He was not massive like Anchorr, but had finer features and jet-black flowing hair. His eyes were as blue as a bubbling brook and his face was as smooth as the lily blossom. The new guardian wore a necklace of golden discs, like the ones in the Hall of Music library, except smaller. He wore shoulder pads that were harps of braided gold and under one arm he carried a curious musical instrument. Now Anchorr was talking to the Master.

"Philyra *(Fə-leer'ə)* is ready, my Lord and King. The Gift is waiting for you inside."

Jesus grasped the Guardian's hand in a powerful man-shake greeting him joyfully.

"Philyra, your assignment is a blessed one, for new life is close to The Creator's heart. You are guarding a promise; and the journey will be one of joy." Then he looked down at Bradey with a perceptive smile and his loving eyes twinkled as he tousled his yellow cherub locks.

"Philyra and the ministering angels are ready to transport our Rainbow. Are you ready to see your mom's face when the Gift arrives?"

"You betcha!" Bradey nearly shouted, mimicking his grandfather's enthusiastic cowboy slang.

Inside the Birthday Palace, the party was in full swing. Happy music was playing from a large stage against one wall. The musicians were radiant youths, and the dancers were beautiful young girls dressed in all the colors of a pastel rainbow. Sarah was among them, leading the dance in a long, lavender gown. Her shiny auburn hair was twisted down her back and tied with lavender ribbons and white baby roses. Servers in lavender and green costumes with crisp, white caps were moving among the crowd with trays of bite-sized delicacies. They were white and fluffy, each bejeweled with a tiny edible rose of pink, yellow, lavender or peach. The palace was full of people laughing and talking together, ooing and aahing over the party décor and activities.

On another platform in the center of the room, a choir of singing cherubs quite close to Bradey's size lifted their tiny voices in song. They were all different from each other but dressed alike in white robes with pink, lavender, blue or green sashes. Their faces shone with smiles as they sang, standing in a semi-circle around a golden pedestal in the center of the round platform. The music of the cherubs was perfectly blended with the instruments and the dancers on the other stage, filling the palace with beautiful harmony. These sights and sounds filled Bradey Josheb with wonder, yet one mystery remained for him. A bright white cushion with a silky pink bow sat on the golden pedestal around which the cherub choir sang. On top of it sat a tiny gold crown, and *something* inside the little tiara emitted burst after burst of rainbow-colored light in perfect rhythm with the music around it.

Bradey inched closer to the round platform, his heavenly curiosity temporarily getting the best of him; but suddenly two dazzling angels with long golden locks and flowing robes took places on the front corners of the main stage and raised curved silver horns to their lips, sounding a series of short, high notes to bring the people to attention. Immediately following the horn duet, another angel, even more stunning than the first two stood between them with arms raised upward.

THE LITTLEST WARRIOR

Bradey saw that the angel had a quiver on his back that was full of arrows; some were gold, some were silver and some were bronze. The angel began to sing with a strong clear voice as the musicians, the cherub choir, and all the people in the palace joined the anthem.

"Praise God from whom all blessings flow!" Bradey realized that the words to this song were in his head, and he could have joined in as well; but he was so enraptured by the goings on of this place that he just stood in awe, taking in every awesome detail. "Praise Him above ye Heavenly hosts;..."

Suddenly, someone shuffled through the crowd and sidled up next to him, saying, all out of breath, "Hey, Bradey! I finally found you! These Special Delivery celebrations are always packed!" It was Robert, holding a beautifully carved, silver yacht. It was delicate and petite; it had *Rainbow* etched on one side and a dainty pink rose on the tip of the bow. He pointed to the glowing angel in front, and explained.

"That's Simcha *(Sim-ka)*, Angel of Joy. He comes to all the delivery festivals. Watch! This is super cool!"

At that moment the song ended and Simcha turned to face the back of the stage, picking up a large bow at his feet. Drawing a silver arrow from the quiver on his back, he placed it on the bow and took aim. Just as Bradey thought he would shoot it into the wall, Simcha gave a great shout.

"Children are the heritage of the Lord!"

Suddenly the wall peeled open to reveal a crystal blue sky filled with soft pink clouds. The two angels with horns raised their instruments for a peal of harmonious notes as Simcha's silver arrow pierced through the atmosphere and sailed out into the clouds below. At the same time, Sarah stepped toward the portal and opened the jeweled lid of a silver box, releasing three dazzling white doves which flew swiftly after the silver arrow into the crystal blue, bearing gifts. The tiny gifts were wrapped sweetly and hung from silk ribbons around their necks. Bradey was fascinated!

Then the crowd began to stir behind Bradey and he turned to see that King Jesus was coming toward him. Bradey had not realized that—during the ceremony—he had inched closer and closer to the round, center stage where the cherubs sang and the golden pedestal stood with the white cushion that held the mysterious tiny crown. But just as Jesus reached him, a shallow golden staircase unfolded from the edge of the platform, stopping at Jesus' feet on the shiny marble floor. Bradey flashed a priceless smile up at his Lord, and King Jesus acknowledged the cherub's excitement with a low chuckle and that same curious twinkle in his eyes. Then he took Bradey's small hand in his very large one and spoke with great pleasure.

"Come, child. Let's send off your Rainbow."

Bradey's heart was pounding now, as they ascended the five stairs to the round platform. The palace hall had become very quiet, except for three large harps that played softly on the music stage behind Simcha. Arriving at the top of the stairs, Jesus stepped up to the golden pedestal and took the white cushion in his hands, lowering it down for Bradey to see. In the center of the small golden crown was a tiny, bright, glittering rainbow with more colors than Bradey had imagined.

THE LITTLEST WARRIOR

With the greatest delight, the King of Heaven said softly, "You may hold your Rainbow for a moment, if you wish."

With a little shiver and a lot of excitement, Bradey slipped one chubby hand around each side of the tiny crown and brought the little rainbow to his chest, peering lovingly at his mother's gift. With each rhythmic beat of his heart, the little rainbow responded with a little fountain of colorful light—almost as if it had a heart of its own. Bending his curly head slightly forward, he touched his little rainbow with his rosy, cherub lips; and was so overcome with joy that all he could think of to say was,

"God bless you, Little Rainbow! And God bless my mother, too!"

Jesus took the gift from Bradey then and held it gently in the palm of his hands, drawing it close to his own heart. Looking upward into the sky blue portal through which Simcha had shot his arrow, Jesus began to bless the little rainbow that would soon be on its way to Earth. And as his voice grew louder and stronger and more passionate, the music began to swell once again, and the people and angels began to lift their voices with Him in joyous praise to God the Father and Heaven's King. As Jesus finished the last words of His blessing upon Bradey's Rainbow, Simcha and all the angels and musicians and dancers on the stage stepped aside and the band of Ministering Angels stepped to the center, while Philyra himself came to the edge of the round center stage and stood at attention before the Lord.

"I send you with my blessing," Jesus concluded with immeasurable love in his calm, clear voice, and tears of great joy in his wonderful eyes. "You will bring joy and song wherever you go. You will shine my light and remember always the sound of my voice. Peace and Safety will go before you, little one that I love."

Slowly, and tenderly, he bent low and placed the white cushion in Philyra's waiting arms; then he kissed the little rainbow and laid the miniature tiara gently on the pillow.

Philyra stepped quickly across the room to the main stage and resolutely climbed the stairs to the stage floor. Six ministering angels split into two rows of three, lining up behind Philyra as he moved to the edge of the portal and stretched his arms forward, poised to fly. In the blink of an eye, Philyra launched into the blue with the band of angels at his heels, and in an instant they were out of sight. The crowd in the palace hall was stone still, and Bradey was totally captivated, as the bright blue with puffy pink clouds faded into the deep expanse of a starry universe. Not a whisper escaped in the elegant room, as a tiny light appeared far away and began to grow. Slowly the yellow glow peeled back to reveal an earthly scene below.

The King reached down and lifted the cherub into his strong arms, whispering close to his ear.

"Watch closely now. Your rainbow has arrived."

Bradey's wide brown eyes were glued to the portal as his sweet mother's tired face came into view. A large hand rested on her shoulder, which he supposed was his dad's. His little brow crinkled as he wondered why his mom looked so tired and so happy at the same time; but as the scene unfolded to show his mother's arms draped in a soft cotton gown, he saw that she cradled a tiny baby close to her heart. Bradey was speechless and full of questions; but Jesus answered before he asked.

THE LITTLEST WARRIOR

"Well, Bradey; there's your rainbow; safe in your mother's arms. Is she happy? What do you think?"

"Yes," Bradey faltered, with a crooked smile, completely mesmerized by the miracles that the Master carried out so effortlessly. Then he brightened.

"My rainbow is a baby *person*? Awesome! Another brother!" Adoring chuckles sprinkled the room with soft laughter and Jesus, smiling widely, answered,

"No...a baby sister, Bradey Josheb. When you requested a special rainbow, I sent a little Princess this time. Isn't she beautiful?" Jesus gazed lovingly at the scene before them.

At last the realization of all that had taken place since Bradey first stood on Mt. Witness came to bear in his keen little mind. He gazed down upon his family below, seeing all of them together now, and felt very close to them—having been the official requestor of The Little Rainbow! He felt the matchless love of the Master drawing them all together and he felt sure that his earthly family could feel it too, for it was evident by their glowing faces that they were all very pleased. He answered softly then.

"Oh, yes, King Jesus, she is very beautiful. Our little Princess is by FAR the most beautiful rainbow I have seen yet!"

Then, looking full into the Lord's face, he added, "Thank you for taking such good care of my mother."

"As the Master of All, it is my great pleasure to do so. Philyra will be your sister's Guardian. See him there, beside your dad? He smiles with joy because he loves his mission. His name means, *Love of Music*; and – besides surrounding her with peace and safety—he will fill our Rainbow Princess with the music of heaven. This will be a particular delight to your mother's heart; and to mine."

"What about the doves?" Bradey questioned, for he saw them fluttering around the scene as if they waited to deliver the gifts they had brought from Heaven.

"They bear the Gifts of Heaven with which the little one will be endowed, according to God's plan for her life on Earth. See how they gently release them now upon the baby's breast? Your mother and father must first discover them before they can be opened; and when they do, the Holy Spirit will impart to them the necessary wisdom to nurture God's gifts in her life."

As the heavenly throng left the Birthday Palace that day, they chattered happily about the wonderful event they had been privileged to witness: the birth of a baby; new life, new joy, new hope. Heaven, however, being such an exciting and adventurous place, would soon fill their vision with many other celebrations and special activities.

Bradey Josheb, on the other hand, left the Birthday Palace with a memory that would stay in his heart forever; and would take him often to the portal at Mount Witness to see his family and especially his Rainbow Princess. He didn't know it then, but becoming a big brother had actually grown him up a bit. He felt bigger and more important now, and he *was*; for he would begin to see Heaven in a whole new light as God's perfect plan unfolded before him. The Littlest Warrior was moving on.

Bradey Josheb stood very still, peering into the clear water of Ryder's pond. He had come to this place to think many times since the Rainbow Celebration, pondering the wonders of the Heavenly Realm, the future of Time and Eternity, and his place in God's Ultimate Plan. Until now, however, he had not paid much attention to his image, for he had been fascinated by the Australian wildlife here at Ryder's "special spot", as he had called it. The Lord had given this place as a gift to Reece Ryder; and now Bradey glanced around this peaceful water garden at the foot of the hills behind Champion Ranch that reminded his cowboy buddy of his native Australia, his earthly home. Ryder and Bradey had come here often after working their horses at The Royal Corrals. They would sit on a log and talk or toss white stones into the still pool to watch the ripples go in circles across the water. The Master— so characteristic of His perfect love—had taken great care to place some of Ryder's favorite animals there for him to enjoy; and he was very pleased to be able to "show and tell" Bradey about each one.

The human-like laughter of the Kookaburra family usually met them before they got to the pond. They were large, noisy birds with a four inch bill from the island of Tasmania. As the boys pulled off their boots to dip their feet in the clear, clean water the geckos would begin to scurry about, climbing up rock faces with their sticky toe pads and peering down at the boys with their large, yellowish eyes.

Ryder had small geckos, large geckos and flying geckos. Sometimes the flying ones would leap out of nowhere, spreading their webbed toes, legs, and tail to help them glide gracefully through the air across the pond. The boys always laughed when a long tongue would dart out to clean their "specs"—nickname for the transparent membrane that protected the geckos oversized eyeballs. Ryder's favorite was the giant tokay, with pale blue skin and reddish spots, that often scampered from his sunny rock to perch on Reece's shoulder.

The boys never tired of watching the pair of black swans with their 6-foot wingspans come in for a landing from a 50 mile-per-hour flight across heaven's skies to skim into Ryder's pond, making waves that set the lily pads to rocking. Right now, as he glanced sideways, Bradey saw the large nest among the cattails at the water's edge that held eight pale green eggs over which the parents—Penny and Cobb—both hovered busily, awaiting the arrival of their new baby cygnets. Bradey reached in his pocket for some golden grain and tossed it in their direction.

A sudden noise across the pond in the tall gum trees made Bradey look up. It was Gummy the Koala, scampering about the branches on his rough padded paws to get a better look at the kangaroos below.
Bradey spied the white patches on his neck and ears, showing between the green leaves of the tree; and he laughed out loud to see that Gummy had stuffed his cheeks with eucalyptus leaves and was dropping the twigs down on the napping roos below. The jill had decided she had enough teasing, and went about to pocket her joey for a hop around Heaven. Bradey always thrilled to see that she could leap 30 feet in a single bound, even with her baby in her pouch.

These thrilling particulars about God's animal kingdom always brought back to Bradey's memory the words of

Toby Jasper, the stable boy when they had first met, *"Welcome to the Master's Heaven, Bradey. There ain't no better place for boys to be!"*

Bradey stared into the crystal pool again, this time seeing the curly-haired cherub that had entered Heaven's gates that day that seemed so long ago and yet as close as yesterday. Time had passed on planet Earth. Bradey Josheb was very familiar with the Master's Heaven now and had, on many occasions, acted as a guide for other tiny souls who had come home. He had made many, many friends, become very closely connected with family members from generations past, and visited amazing places all over the realm.

Now as he stared solemnly at the image below, he wondered why he had not noticed it before. He had seen his brothers growing on earth, and had been amazed with each visit to the portal on Mount Witness to discover that his little sister was growing from a baby into a tiny little person, very like the cherub he remembered himself to be. Where had that cherub gone?

His brooding came to a sudden halt when Greater grandfather slapped his shoulders and chuckled, stepping up to peer into the pool beside Bradey.

"Well, can ya beat that? I'd throw ya in the pond if you were still a little tyke, but lookee there! Yer almost big enough to throw ME in! Hee-heeee!"

Bradey grinned at Grandpa Doc and said, "When did I get so big, Grandpa? It seems like yesterday that I was riding on your shoulders; and look at Cherub!" Bradey

THE LITTLEST WARRIOR

flung one arm in the direction of his young stallion. "He's almost a full-grown horse!"

Grandpa Doc chuckled merrily and answered, "Well, it's a good thing; 'cause them boots o' yours'd be draggin' the ground if that pony wasn't growin' along with ya, boy!"

A deep, familiar voice called from behind them and they both turned toward the corral.

"That's what I come to tell ya, Bradey-boy," explained Grandpa, turning back to Bradey. "Your Guardian's come lookin' for ya; you've both been summoned to Mount Witness.

Bradey arched his eyebrows in surprise and whistled sharply for Cherub as they turned to walk back. Seeing Anchorr's stern expression, Bradey picked up his pace and hurried to the gate.

"Anchorr, my friend; what's the news?"

"The time has come, my liege!"

Anchorr bowed his head slightly and looked straight into Bradey's eyes with both exhilaration and reluctance, saying no more. Bradey understood immediately and returned his Guardian's unwavering gaze with a firm-lipped smile and eyes of deep appreciation and loyalty, grasping his massive forearm in a strong and heart-felt man-shake.

"Come." Bradey turned to command his pets; Cherub who had trotted to his side and Whisper who was no longer a cuddly ball of fur but a half-grown snow leopard.

The big cat had *str-e-tch-ed* out of his nap on the straw to an alert sitting position, his emerald-green eyes riveted on Bradey. Bradey swung easily onto Cherub's back from the ground and Whisper sprang to his feet, crouching low and watching his master. Without another word, Anchorr moved swiftly across the corral to the outside gate and headed down the ranch path with long, purposeful strides to the Golden Road. Adventure was in the air.

Bradey had a difficult time keeping up with Anchorr's pace, even though Cherub's gait was quick and powerful. His Guardian was so very massive, even compared to many other guardians of the realm. Whisper ran beside him for at least half of the distance but finally ran ahead to climb a tree and then leaped onto Anchorr's broad shoulder to ride the rest of the way. Bradey smiled to think of how Anchorr used to swing him onto his broad shoulders for so many of their treks across the Master's Heaven. A warm devotion spread over him as he thought of Anchorr's loyalty and friendship. They had a bond that could not be described with mere words. He had always known that this day would come, and his heart pounded with great anticipation for Anchorr, but his temporary absence would be acutely felt by many; especially Bradey Josheb, the Littlest Warrior who had been ushered to the Heavenly Realm in Anchorr's capable hands.

Mount Witness was visible now and Cherub's sides heaved with the workout of the steep climb. Anchorr could have flown to the top, but had respectfully held back for the sake of his subject. Bradey could sense his Guardian's intensity, however, and nudged Cherub's sides to encourage more effort still. Whisper, meantime, had been overcome with the jostling of his high perch on Anchorr's shoulder and had leaped to the ground, now loping along beside Cherub and Bradey as if the mountainside was as easily travelled as a flat plain.

Up ahead, a Company of Guardians dressed in battle gear began to assemble under the rainbow at the top of Mount Witness. King Jesus stood in the midst of them looking toward the portal. Bradey wondered what they would see—a breathless shiver going up and down his youthful spine. The King saw them coming and turned his strong gaze toward their small company. Anchorr reached him first and bowed.

"We have come to do your bidding, my Lord." and waited for Bradey to dismount and stand before his Master.

"Here I am, Master; you called."

Jesus took Bradey by the shoulders and looked at him tenderly. "My Littlest Warrior is not so little any more. You have attained numerous levels of experience since entering the Heavenly Realm as a small cherub; but you are no longer a little one. You have grown in knowledge and wisdom, entering the ranks of the Youth of Heaven. I am pleased with your dedication and progress and you are now ready for training." He smiled knowingly at Bradey's instant enthusiasm.

"You have been a delight to many since your arrival; and you have excelled as a companion, a guide, and a fine student. I am pleased with you, Bradey Josheb. Now you must pursue your calling as a mighty warrior of the Heavenly Realm. It is my will that you be enrolled in Yashobam's training camp immediately."

He squeezed Bradey's young shoulders, drawing the boy to his great bosom and holding him tightly. Bradey hugged him back, loving his Lord so completely and wanting nothing more than to please Him and become everything he was created to be from his birth. Then holding him at arm's length and looking at his ruddy face, the Lord nodded toward his Guardian, adding,

"And with your graduation to training level, your faithful guardian, Anchorr, will be re-assigned to Earth."

Releasing the Little Warrior, The Master turned to Anchorr with a quick and powerful man-shake.

"Prepare for battle." In a flash Anchorr was gone.

The portal began to open before the company on the mountain. Cries and groans; deafening explosions accosted Bradey's ears before the scenes of war became visible below. Such a terrible battle ensued on earth! Through the portal, scene after scene from one side of the globe to the other showed hatred and strife; full-scale wars; battles on land and sea. Dog-fights filled the earthly skies with combat; and innumerable small skirmishes covered a multitude of village landscapes with blood and tears. Every conceivable tool of death and destruction was active on the earth below. Bradey was in shock, despite his keen supernatural mind, and watched in horror.

Deeply grieved, the King of Heaven spoke with a quivering voice that demonstrated both heartfelt anguish and strong passion.

"Wars and rumors of wars cover the continents of Earth. Satan and his allies will not rest until the cup of

THE LITTLEST WARRIOR

destruction runs over. His uncontrollable rage has ravished the land in his ferocious effort to kill the bodies and damn the souls of men before they can be redeemed. As we prepare for the Last Battle at the End of Time, war will continue in every corner of the world and many will be lost."

Then, standing tall with arms outstretched he turned to face the huge company of guardians ready to deploy, finishing strongly.

"You are dispatched to answer the cries of my people who suffer on Earth at the hands of my enemies. Go swiftly, each to his post; bolster them with courage to do what is set before them. Strengthen the weary, succor the wounded, and comfort the dying; for some will be called away."

Bradey watched in awe as this massive army of battle-ready guardians stood at attention, saluting their Commander in Chief. He saw now that Anchorr had re-joined the throng, dressed in full battle gear like the others.

His voice of unmatched authority reaching a potent climax that rang across the skies of Heaven, Christ the King shouted, thrusting a powerful fist into the air.

"For the Ultimate Plan and the Glory of God the Father, Thy will be done on Earth as it is in Heaven!"

Poised shields sprang forward and raised swords glittered brilliantly in the Light of the Lamb as a thunderous unified chant rattled the landscape.

"One Cause! One Conqueror! One King!"

COMMISSIONED

Then, in the clattering surge of armor and the mighty rush of a thousand wings, they were gone. But in the cloud of gold dust that rose from the mountain, Bradey was sure he saw the form of his own Anchorr standing tall; saluting his goodbye with one fisted forearm across his heart and the other raised powerfully skyward. Then he was gone; and Bradey's youthful brown eyes stung with honor and joy.

Bradey and The King stood motionlessly for some time, captivated by the power and the glory of the moment. Bradey had always been enraptured by the stories of the Guardians; and he would be forever thrilled that the same great one that was commissioned to service for the famous Yashobam of old—one of King David's mightiest men—had been assigned to *him*! How many other great warriors would join the ranks of Anchorr's subjects before the end of time? Anchorr had waited for this day.

"Let's go, Bradey," the gentle voice of the Savior of the World interrupted his thoughts. Taking Cherub's bridal he turned to the Lord as they began their decent.

"I am constantly amazed at the power and precision of your plan. To think that three realms of such great diversity are now swirling in Time and Eternity—the heavenly, the hellish, and the earthly—and yet with each moment that passes, your will is being accomplished and your ultimate victory is already won!"

Jesus smiled lovingly as he listened to Bradey's heart, and was filled with joy at his understanding of the Plan of the Ages. Now his attention turned to the bottom of the last hill where someone waited with two fresh horses, one of which Bradey recognized unmistakably as The Champion.

"Bradford!" The Lord called from up the hill. "Thank you for coming. I've been watching for you!"

Bradey did not know who this person was, but he was about to be pleasantly surprised. As the last slope of the foothills flowed into the flat grasslands below Mount Witness, a tall, muscular man stepped forward with a broad smile, handing Champion's reigns to The Master. Then the Lord turned to Bradey.

"You have discovered by now that your earthly relations are numerous in my kingdom, haven't you? You have met many who lived generations before you were born and, although there are no generation gaps in Heaven, this one was very close to your world. Meet your Great-uncle Bradford!"

Bradey's dimpled grin met the uncle's firm man-shake. As he pulled the boy into a strong embrace, Bradey smelled leather and fire—distinguishing traces from the camps of heaven's warriors. Bradey's nostrils flared involuntarily and with a sudden burst of heavenly adrenaline he remembered the manly destination for which he was presently bound.

King Jesus mounted Champion and waved, giving instructions to Bradey.

"Your first assignment in training will be as your uncle's apprentice in weapons design. He is my Weapons Master at the training camp. He will teach you well." Then Champion reared up on his hind legs and they were off; sprinting across the meadow.

"I hear you learn quickly;" the uncle grinned at Bradey. "That's good because I move fast. Mount up, nephew; we have work to do."

Then sidling up to Cherub, he added, nodding toward his own horse, "This is Vigor; and you can call me Chazz."

"Why Chazz?" Bradey questioned with a quizzical grin.

"Because," his uncle answered. "It means **Free Man**; and that, my boy, is what I am."

Then he was off in a gallop across the meadow with Bradey on Cherub following close behind, and Whisper—not loping along this time—turning on high gear to keep up. Bradey hadn't ridden Cherub this fast for a long time and it was exhilarating to feel the wind whipping his long, wavy hair; for it was no longer a crop of short curly-Qs around a cherub face. The image in Ryder's pond that had surprised him so was of a youth—about 15 in human years—with clear bronze skin and thick, blonde hair just past his shoulders, but shorter around his strong young face. He had large hands and fine but masculine features; dark brows and thick lashes lined his large brown eyes prominently and his jaw was square and chiseled, softened only by the deep dimples that framed his striking smile.

Two young boys threw the gates open wide as Bradey and Uncle Chazz walked their horses into camp. Bradey was full of heavenly adrenaline as he took in the sites with wide eyes. He felt like a rushing river was coursing through his veins. He glanced back at the boys by the gate and their eyes met. They smiled and waved. He remembered them. He had met them at Kid's Paradise; now he understood the connection he had felt with them back then; they must have been called as warriors, too.

Outside the armory, two stable boys took the horses away to brush, feed and water them, while Whisper began to prowl around the camp and make friends with other young warriors. Uncle Chazz took Bradey on a tour of the armory where all the weapons of war were stored and showed him the fascinating process of building them, from start to finish. There was a bright room with a huge skylight for a ceiling where design tables were set up in the center and many and varied tools and measuring instruments lined the walls. Men were busily working with some of the tools at several of the tables, but Bradey and Chazz stopped at one along the edge of the design area that was clearly unused.

"This is where you will learn weapons design," Uncle Chazz stated matter-of-factly.

He kept moving and Bradey could hardly keep up, let alone stop to ask questions. They toured the Metals Shop and the Soldering Rooms, where Bradey instantly recognized the smell of fire he had encountered on his uncle's clothing when they first met. He marveled at the King's bountiful riches in the Vault where gold, silver and precious stones were stored. Then they saw the Stonecutter's Courtyard where gems were shaped for embedding into hilts, sheaths, blades and many other pieces of battle dress and gear. There was no shortage of riches here; and every piece of equipment created for the Armies of Heaven was studded with jewels and embossed with the symbols of the Lion and the Lamb.

A trumpet blared somewhere in the center of the camp and Bradey's uncle turned to explain.

"Yashobam calls the troops together now. You will have several introductory sessions with him and then you will rest, eat and fellowship with the troops. After that I will meet you back at the design gallery to begin your apprenticeship." With a man-shake and a nod he added, "Glad to have you, nephew. I'll see you soon; that way, to Yashobam."

Bradey turned to see many other youths heading toward the center of camp, so he followed the general direction of their movement and came to a large semi-circle of log benches facing a stone-slab platform. He recognized Yashobam immediately and found a seat on the front row. He would finally get to know his God-ordained mentor and learn to follow in the footsteps of a true warrior; one of the greatest who had ever walked the earth. Watching Yashobam so intently, Bradey did not realize that three other youths had taken seats on the same row to his left, until he heard someone say,

"Hello. My name is Iniko." He was very dark-skinned with short kinky hair. His sober chocolate eyes and slightly broad nose were handsome features but insignificant in the light of his prominent white smile.

"Bradey," he nodded and extended a man-shake.

"I am Sheng Li," the next boy down initiated with an extended hand. He was oriental with fine features and dark eyes that matched the jet black hair cropped just above his shoulders. Bradey noticed that he had an iron grip, though he was slight-built and wiry. They clasped forearms.

Bradey started to lean forward around the other two to meet the third youth, but the boy stood and stepped toward him, so Bradey stood also and spoke to him.

"Bradey Josheb," he said with a nod. The man-shake was powerful between them, and head-on, locking in a mysterious connection that Bradey had felt the first time he saw this boy.

"Uzi [oo-zee] Seth-Kenan Zacharee," he said with a calm but passionate tone. His green-hazel eyes were striking beneath thick dark brows against his very olive skin, and his hair was dark brown and wavy; brushed away from his face and curling into loose, short ringlets down the back of his neck. "Call me Uzi," he added grinning with one side of his mouth. Bradey nodded with his notorious deep-dimpled smile, as Uzi took his place on Bradey's right.

A loud clashing of swords on the stone platform caused all eyes to be riveted forward. Two warriors in full battle gear stood poised for a fencing match. The contest began immediately and the youths were spellbound with every intense detail. The warriors seemed evenly matched in skill, but finally the larger of the two triumphed, pinning the other in a corner with the edge of the sword at his neck. Shouts of boyish adrenaline whooping their approval of the show filled the atmosphere with electric expectation as Yashobam took the stage.

"You are here to learn the ways of war," he began in his booming voice. Then, as the winner of the joust removed his helmet to revel a surprisingly fair face, Yashobam motioned for him to come.

"This is Grant Finlay; on Earth, a Scot and a knight; in Heaven, the Great Fair Warrior, as his name depicts so well."

Finlay bowed slightly, looking like a tank in his get-up; his nearly white-blonde hair was wet around his face and neck from the workout but his massive chest heaved only slightly.

He is a giant! Bradey thought, admiring this big man's skill and brawn.

Yashobam continued, "Finlay is the camp Weapons Mentor; he will teach you to use the weapons of war with great skill. He is a Master; watch him and learn."

Having the rapt attention of the ranks of Heaven's Youth, Yashobam introduced himself as their primary instructor and gave an overview of the classes.

"Our primary objective is service; we live and breathe and fight for the honor and glory of the Lamb; the King of Heaven. Thus our slogan, *One Cause; One Conqueror; One King!* We are brothers in all things; linking arms in learning, in practice, and in victory; receiving with honor and humility our great commission in the service of the King of Kings."

The hearts of the young men who listened beat proud as each one identified himself with the purpose and the power of their mission, hanging on every word of their leader.

"A warrior's first responsibility is worship; this is Course I. Knowledge is next; you will be immersed in the Truth of our God and King—His Eternal Word, His Timeless Purpose, and His Everlasting Kingdom. Skill building will follow your foundational courses. Your classes will include: Fitness and Riding; Tools and Weaponry, and Battle Strategies. You will watch the greatest battles in History from The Chronicles of Time amphitheater; and you will meet the greatest warriors who ever lived to serve Christ the King!"

His voice rose throughout his speech, in power and passion, ending with a shout that brought cheers from the enamored young warriors. Then Yashobam's voice took on a low but commanding tone.

"And you," he pointed with an authoritative gesture, "have been chosen—individually by His Majesty—to take part in the greatest battle of all Time and Eternity." His volume increased slightly. "The Final Battle!" and increased significantly more, "and Ultimate Victory!" And then with a mighty shout and both burly arms high in the air he shouted, "of the LION... of Judah!"

A tumult of triumphant shouts joined in the air above the small arena then as the young enthusiasts leaped from their bench seats clapping and stomping and chanting in unison.

"One CAUSE!   One CONQUEROR!   One KING!" over and over again.

Then the worship of the heavenly hosts—heard at all times throughout The Kingdom, since they worshipped continually around the Throne of God, but at significant intervals becoming much more prominent—suddenly filled the skies above Camp Conquest with a glorious roar.

"Worthy is the Lamb that was slain to receive power, and riches, and wisdom, and strength, and honor and glory, and blessing!"

Yashobam bellowed at the top of his lungs, as a blinding light brought him to his brawny knees, "Behold, The Lamb!"

A hush fell over the young crowd then as they saw The Master in all his brilliant glory before them—not as their friend with loving eyes and constant affection, although he was that; not as the crowned epitome of highest royalty, although he was most certainly that; not even as their Savior with those eternally significant nail-scarred hands, although—their Savior he would forever be. Just now, they saw the Lord of All in a new light: with eyes of fire and a blazing sword; with a fearsome, even formidable, expression of holy vengeance; they saw Him now as a figure of impenetrable power; the ultimate, unstoppable warrior; inevitable Victor—the Lord Jesus Christ, their Commander in Chief.

Falling prostrate before him, this little band of warriors-in-training was instantly reduced from a group of confident, boisterous young boys to a solemn, silent company of modest young men.

"Arise," the voice of the Lord was like thunder this time, reverberating the very ground on which they lay. To one knee they arose as a unit, heads bowed; fisted arms across their chests in heart-felt devotion.

Extending a flaming sword over the new troops, the Ultimate Warrior spoke again; his voice echoed in their ears.

"I commission you into the Ranks of Heavenly Warriors; to the glory of God the Father, to the honor of God the Son; to the power of God the Holy Spirit. I AM has sent you to vanquish his enemies; to carry out

THE LITTLEST WARRIOR

his will on Earth as it is in Heaven; to unite his Eternal Kingdom. Onward, in the name of Christ your King!"

He was gone from their midst in an instant, and after a long silence the deep voice of Yashobam drew all eyes to the front. He was smiling broadly now, fairly beaming, actually; for this band of little brothers had been inducted into the ranks of the mightiest of men, and he was proud to have witnessed their Commission.

"Welcome to the Armies of Heaven!"

Training Camp

After Yashobam's introduction and the commissioning of the young recruits, Grant Finlay took them on a complete tour of Camp Conquest. It was a young man's dream. The camp was laid out like a giant triangle with Worship, Study, and Weaponry in each of the three corners. Inside this large triangle was a smaller one that formed the Troops Quarters. Yashobam had called them to the Rally Stage which was a tight circle in the bull's-eye of the camp; the Troop Quarters Triangle was around it. One corner of the Troop QT was like a chow hall, one was a rest area, and one was a place for meditation. Finlay had pointed out all these things and then led them out of the Troop QT past the rest area and across a field toward the Worship Point.

This area faced the center of the Heavenly Realm, pointing toward the Throne of God. Finlay explained that all the worship of Heaven flowed toward The Father's House and surrounded his throne. There was a small rushing stream that ran in front of a wide gold and ivory stairway. Three small bridges led over the water to the stairs and each had a gate inscribed with a name.

"The Names of God are inscribed on every gate you will see in this camp;" explained Finlay as he approached the gated bridges.

"These three are El Elyon, El Shaddai, and Yaweh Melek—our Sovereign God, our Comfort, our King. This stream is a tributary from the River of Life that runs through the Heavenly Realm, and across these bridges the stairs will lead you to the Pinnacle of High Praise where you will learn to worship the Most High."

Bradey's heart thrilled when he saw a glimpse of the platform at the top of the stairs. The Pinnacle was so high that he was sure the view of the entire kingdom would be fantastic from up there. Even though he knew there was a lot to learn about worship, he felt a song in his heart and was already bursting with praise to God the Father. The boys wanted to run across the bridges and climb the stairs. Grant Finlay laughed at their great enthusiasm.

"Every true warrior has a heart of worship," he explained; "and I appreciate your zeal but we will finish the tour of the camp before we begin our activities." He turned back toward the field they had just come across.

"This is where your training exercises will take place. The Training Field surrounds the Troop QT. As we walk around the edges, we will come to each of the training points. This is the Worship Point; one of three key training areas."

Then he was on the move again, and they followed eagerly. They left the Worship Gates and walked along the edge of the Training Field toward the next area which was the Word Point. The boys chattered excitedly as they looked out across the field and wondered what kinds of activities their field training would include. Approaching the structure where their Truth Studies would take place, Bradey noticed that it was a great pyramid. The two sides that he could see as his company came closer had four large star-shaped window-openings; he assumed there were four windows on the third side as well, and wondered what could be inside the massive walls. Along the front, the boys saw five arched doorways, each inscribed with another name. Grant Finlay passed two doors named Yaweh Ro'i and El Olam, stopping in front of the middle doorway, Yaweh Maccaddeschem, and began to explain, reaching high to trace a line under the long title with his spear.

"God, our Sanctifier, has set each of us apart for His purposes. This is where you will discover your part in that purpose."

Pointing back toward the two doors they had passed, he repeated the names above each one with their meanings.

"Yaweh Ro'i, our shepherd; El Elyon, Sovereign and Supreme." Then pointing toward the two doors at the other end he continued. "Jehovah Ropheka; Jehovah Tsidkenu; God our Healer; God our Righteousness, without whom we can do nothing."

Then he pushed the middle door open with his massive forearm and the troops followed him into a high ceilinged lecture hall. When they were all inside and grouped around him, Grant Finlay spoke again.

"Each of the five outer doors leads to a classroom like this one where great scholars from all ages past will teach you the ways of God and His Plan of the Ages. As you learn the elements of His nature and the essentials of His Ultimate Plan, your spirits will be enlarged." He thumped his broad chest with a thick fist for emphasis.

"As your spirits grow, your knowledge and abilities will expand and you will acquire the wisdom of experienced warriors. Many of your mentors bear the scars of the earthly battles that they fought against the enemies of God. Much of what they have acquired in wisdom, knowledge and skill was gained through fierce combat and many human mistakes. But you have been called as Heavenly Warriors. Your training takes place in the Heavenly Realm, but you will see battle on the earth, for you are being prepared to march with the Armies of Heaven to an earthly conquest—the Last Battle, and the greatest, of all Time and Eternity."

Silence reigned as the young recruits stared wide-eyed, hanging on every word that Grant Finlay spoke. They felt the zeal of God pounding in their chests, and their hearts swelled with the honor of the Call. They felt the brotherhood of camaraderie, the strength of their mission and a rushing, powerful surge of confidence and invincibility—undoubtedly the super-version of male adrenaline. They were budding warriors—from head to toe.

Opening a double door at the back of the lecture hall, Finlay exposed a central antechamber into which all five classrooms led. This curious atrium was a 50 foot cylinder with a translucent glass ceiling that glowed with peculiar light. The high walls were covered with hand and foot holds, and ledges at various heights for climbing. Finlay allowed the boys to investigate; grinning from ear to ear as they tried to figure out this mysterious hall. Then, pointing up toward the edges of the ceiling, he explained further.

"Those openings go into the auditorium where we will gather for assemblies of the Council of Warriors. When you go to assembly, you will climb these walls to enter. This is part of your training. Let's see how you do."

The boys whooped and hollered as they tried their climbing skills on the cylinder walls; but try as they might, they could only climb a few feet before they fell clumsily to the floor. A circle of long ropes hung from a thick copper halo at the top of the cylinder. Grant Finlay grabbed one of the thick ropes and began climbing hand over hand, scaling the distance in no time. The boys were in awe of his great strength as he quickly reached the top, 50 feet up, and pulled himself through an opening to the room above. Laughing heartily at their surprise, he shouted down to them.

"When you learn the secret of a warrior's strength, you will all be able to do the same! Now, hit the stairs!"

Finding a narrow staircase winding upwards on one side of the wall, the boys bounded single file to the lofty second floor of the pyramid; entering a plush theater of tiered seats with royal blue cushions. The floor resembled thick, blown glass blocks full of tiny bubbles; its muted colors swirled in beautiful patterns that veiled the depths of the cylinder below while still emitting a soft glow, the source of the chamber's peculiar light. The narrow openings around the edge of the glass floor were marked by short, stout rails—just over a foot high and about twice as wide—made of brushed silver bars to provide grips for the climbers entering from the antechamber below.

The front of the auditorium was a marble and copper platform where twelve oversized silver chairs were placed in a slight semi-circle. They had velvet-padded seats, backs, and armrests of royal blue, golden yellow and deep red with silver piping. A massive replica of Moses' tablets of stone dominated the stage wall behind the platform. It was engraved with the Ten Commandments; and a velvet banner of royal blue and

THE LITTLEST WARRIOR

crimson red was displayed above with words of gold: *Yaweh Shaphat: Our Judge* and *Jehovah Chaqaq: Our Lawgiver*. Finlay was speaking.

"The warriors of this Council are many and mighty. They are men of distinction—prophets, kings, soldiers and apostles of the faith who have earned their ranks through dedicated service to the Lord of All. We will come regularly to hear them speak. You will thrill at the stories they tell, and learn much from every experience they share. They are your mentors in the Battle of the Ages which will culminate in the great War of all Wars, at the End of Time. They will often watch your training exercises and monitor your progress in order to address particular skills or strategies. Listen well, and follow their counsel."

As the young recruits descended the staircase to the ground floor of the pyramid, Bradey's mind was racing. His heart pounded at the thought of seeing and hearing the great warriors of the past, and studying under their tutelage. Though he had not met them, he already admired them for their dedication to God and His Ultimate Plan during the evident difficulties of their earthly pilgrimages. How privileged he was to learn from so many seasoned warriors.

Standing outside once again, Bradey scanned the scenes in front of him. He had waited for this day—the day that he would begin his training as a Warrior of the Heavenly Realm. Now he was here, with others who had been called to do the same. The atmosphere was electric with anticipation.

Catching up to the group, Bradey saw the Weapons Point up ahead, where Uncle Chazz directed weapons design and assembly. Yaweh Sabbaoth – Commander of Heaven's Armies – was inscribed on the Weapons Gate, which looked like a great shield with two massive spears for gate posts. Pausing at the gate, Finlay exhorted the young men once again about the honor and privilege of their commission in the greatest army of all time under the Lord of Hosts, Christ the King.

Inside, Grant showed them the Metals Shop and the Smoldering Rooms to the left, the Armory and the Design Gallery to the right, with the Stonecutter's Courtyard in between. Finally, they entered the Vault at the back where enormous mounds of gold, silver and precious stones were stored for the final embellishments of Heaven's weaponry. Bradey had already toured the weapons site with Uncle Chazz; but he got the same shivers up and down his youthful spine as he had the first time.

Weapons, without doubt, will trigger an adrenaline rush for any warrior; but there was no end to the questions and excitement generated by seeing the process of designing and creating them. The electric atmosphere produced by the boys' enthusiasm and anticipation made it difficult for Grant Finlay to herd them from area to area in an orderly manner; although their compliance, as youths of The Kingdom, was unquestionable.

In the Armory, they were each allowed to choose a weapon to hold and examine. Uncle Chazz had joined their party at the gate so he could assist Finlay in the tour. He encouraged the boys to ask questions, and answered every one of them with the knowledge of a master craftsman and skillful warrior. The boys were intrigued, and could have stood there all day holding those elements of war—if, in fact, there had been such a

THE LITTLEST WARRIOR

thing as "a day" in Heaven. Instead, time was of no concern to anyone.

Their next exhilarating opportunity came in the Metals Shop where skilled craftsmen mentored them through the simple process of creating an armband. They each chose a strip of either bronze or platinum, which was fitted to their right upper arm. Next, they were allowed to experiment with some of the tools on scrap metal, while the master craftsmen engraved their names on the bands. Then they proceeded to the Soldering Rooms where brass discs were imprinted with emblems by using tools that resembled branding irons. The boys could choose the image of the Lion or the Lamb. Both mascots wore a crown and had the words *"One King"* inscribed beneath the head. These embellished ornaments were then soldered to the top edge of the armbands. The youths were enraptured by every detail of the process and donned their new bands with great decorum. This experience created a solemn, unifying sentiment that began to stir a profound loyalty deep within their spirits. They were sensing the strength of moving as one; embracing the passion of devoted brotherhood. They entered the courtyard as a unified troop; a band of brothers marching to the drumbeat of the Master's call.

In the Stonecutter's Courtyard, craftsmen were busy faceting gems of all sizes, shapes and colors for embedding into sword hilts, scabbards, shields and body armor. These precious stones would very often catch a glinting ray of the Light of the Lamb and send prisms of color dancing along the courtyard walls. It was a beautiful sight to behold; and what was even more remarkable was the rich music that resonated from this place. The deep, melodious voices of the craftsmen who worked so joyfully with the Master's gems boomed forth songs of praise about the Rock of Ages; lauding He who is more precious than silver and more costly than gold; exalting the One whose worth is more than all costly treasures combined. Filing past the Vault of precious stones, the young warriors were obliged to recognize the truth of the craftsmen's songs. For though the piles of gems glistened with magnificent splendor through the open gate, none flashed so brightly as the twinkle they had seen in their Master's eyes, nor shone so purely as the holy light surrounding his kingly being. While nothing on earth would ever compare to the riches of Heaven, still, nothing in Heaven could compare to its King.

Following the exhilarating tour of the training compound, the boys were encouraged to take positions of repose in the troops quarters Rest Area. Some lounged on the grass; some reclined against walls, or lay on their backs with feet up on a bench, taking in the clear skies of Heaven and basking in the warmth of its Light. Their boyish souls were filled with tranquility as the voices of Heaven's Realm joined together across the atmosphere to honor The King; their praise bringing the perfect balance of worship to galvanize each warrior's heart of dedication to His Cause.

The paradisiacal version of a soldier's mess hall was crowded with eager young warriors and busy servers with tray upon tray of scrumptious dishes. Bradey stood just inside the door, taking in the scene. A hand waving across the room caught his attention as Iniko's broad, white smile flashed a warm welcome above the sea of young faces. Bradey made his way through the crowded hall to the table where his three new friends sat with plates of steaming food.

THE LITTLEST WARRIOR

"This food is much better than the rice and tea of my earthly home;" Sheng Li said before stuffing his mouth with a big, juicy chunk of roast beef—the divine version, that is. Bradey stabbed a piece of meat on the serving platter just before a server took it away and replaced it with another dish.

"What's rice?" Bradey asked innocently. The others laughed.

"It is similar to that, actually;" Uzi gestured toward the newest platter of steaming food.

"Except," Iniko chimed in, "removing the colorful vegetables and good flavor and throwing a few bugs into the mix!" The other three boys laughed heartily.

Bradey was not in on the joke, never having tasted third-world rice—and certainly not bugs; and, therefore, not understanding their comparison with this fluffy, aromatic and flavorful rendition of this apparently common earthly food. He grinned unreservedly, however, realizing that his companions had undoubtedly experienced many things during their earthly pilgrimages that he may never understand. The only food he had ever tasted was the rich recipes of the Heavenly Realm, although it would take an eternity to sample them all.

"What is your favorite food?" he asked, glancing around the table. Just then a server came by with a tray of serving dishes piled high with a sublime variant of candied yams. Bradey, spying the toasted marshmallows on top, recognized something he knew he liked and snatched a pan for their table as the server edged around his chair.

"Thank you, sir," he grinned at the man, who nodded and chuckled merrily.

"There are too many to name," Uzi answered first; "and I'm sure this will be another one!" He reached for the spoon and gave the others a heap of sweet yams before serving himself. "Eat up, lads! We will soon be taking our exercise on the Training Field!"

Their first exercises were packed with strength training, weapons handling and combat skills. Outside the camp, they mounted horses for races, jumping exercises and obstacle courses. Their schedule was rigorous and—for what would have been weeks or months on Earth—they moved continually among the classrooms at Word Point, the Weapons Corner, and the various training fields; with regular intervals in between for rest, food, and personal meditation at the Troops Quarters. Also interspersing their many activities were numerous calls to worship where the sound of a ram's horn would call them to the Worship Gates. They would file over the bridges and up the giant staircase, following their leaders in interactive hymns of praise; and finally at the top, from the Pinnacle of High Praise, they would lift their young masculine voices in resounding corporate worship toward Heaven Central and the Father's Throne.

Bradey Josheb loved to stand on the very edge of the platform that crowned the Pinnacle—since there was no fear of falling in Heaven—with his arms outstretched. Lifting his strong baritone voice Bradey Josheb would pilot the young warriors' chorus of praise. He was becoming a leader, unbeknown to him, and would often on these occasions, as the worship subsided, turn his face upward and make a fist with both hands. Then he would pull his arms down swiftly into a flexed position, making every muscle ripple like rocks under his bronze skin, and shout.

"We are stronger than before!" Turning to face his peers, he would cross his forearms over his heart and add with true conviction "Every facet of our being is energized when we give ourselves to worship."

After the third occurrence of this passionate display, his fellow-warriors began to follow his example. As soon as they saw him tip his face to the sky, letting his wavy golden locks fall past his shoulder blades, they would all clinch their fists for the power stroke, following his lead and crossing their hearts as one. Then they would thrust their right fists in the air three times as they shouted their motto in unison.

"One Cause! One Conqueror! One King!"

The days and years went by on Earth below as Heaven's young warriors honed their supernatural skills. They had all mastered the climb up the cylinder's 50-ft. walls—although none had been able to replicate Finlay's arm-over-arm rope climbing feat to the top—and they had attended many assemblies with the Council of Warriors. Line upon line, precept upon precept, they were learning the ways of God and the strategies of spiritual warfare. During one such assembly, King David of old spoke to them about the human heart; the struggle between flesh and spirit; and his hard lessons on earth in becoming a man after God's own heart. Then he delighted them by taking them on a fieldtrip to the Chronicles of Time and Eternity, where Bradey had first sat as a cherub in the lap of The Master to learn the History of the World.

King David called up the Old Testament story of his boyhood in the hills of Bethlehem, as he kept his father's sheep day after day. The young men sat on the edges of their seats in the gallery as they witnessed scene after scene: David killing the lion; David killing the bear; David playing his harp in worship to God; David challenging the Philistine army and killing their giant with a sling and five stones.

Each heart beat strong as the youths vicariously experienced the thrill of David's victories. They felt his anointing in their own bosoms as his youthful voice from the past shouted down Goliath in the power of the Spirit.

"You come to me with a sword, with a spear, and with a javelin. But I come to you in the name of the Lord of hosts, the God of the armies of Israel, whom you have defied. This day the Lord will deliver you into my hand, and I will strike you and take your head from you. And this day I will give the carcasses of the camp of the Philistines to the birds of the air and the wild beasts of the earth, that all the earth may know that there is a God in Israel. Then all this assembly shall know that the Lord does not save with sword and spear; for the battle is the Lord's, and He will give you into our hands." (I Samuel 17:45-47 NKJV™)

And when the giant fell with a crash to the ground, the young company of onlookers leaped to their feet and gave a shout of victory for the young shepherd of Israel. As the scene grew dark and then faded into Heaven's blue, King David stood before the rows of young warriors in the gallery and dismissed them with a final exhortation.

THE LITTLEST WARRIOR

"There were many other times in my life when I compromised my position by forgetting that the battle was the Lord's. When the Spirit of the Lord comes upon a man, he is no longer just a man; he becomes a powerful, supernatural weapon against the enemies of Almighty God. And as long as he remembers who he is, and who he is not, he will succeed, to the glory of the Lamb."

The boys began to stand, stretch and talk among themselves, but Bradey sat mesmerized by the truth that had suddenly hit a chord deep in his spirit; and he whispered to himself the words he had heard in one form or another from every mighty man that had addressed them in the Council or in classes: *"... 'Not by might nor by power, but by my Spirit,' says the Lord Almighty."*

"That's it...that's it!" he shouted, jumping to his feet; and he leaped over two rows of seats in the galley and headed for the camp in a dead run. He was fast; and the only peers who could keep up with him were Iniko and Uzi, who were close on his heels. They didn't know what had gotten into him; but they weren't about to miss it.

Now, The Chronicles amphitheater was quite a long ways from the camp; and if human eye could have seen these young men race down the mountain it would easily be compared to the prophet Elijah who, anointed with God's power, had raced King Ahab's chariot down Mount Carmel in a rainstorm and beat him to the entrance of Jezreel. They ran as if they were flying, and burst through the gate with the zeal of Olympians. Bradey sprinted to the Word Gate, Maccaddeshem, and paused before entering.

"My God, my Sanctifier, who has set me apart for your eternal purpose," he spoke with reverence and zeal.

Iniko and Uzi followed as he headed through the first classroom to the central atrium. They looked at each other with heaving chests from the strenuous run, wondering what Bradey was doing. He stood in the center of the cylinder staring up at the glass ceiling; then he looked at his companions with the light of new dawn on his face and said with a passionate tone.

"I know the secret! Did you hear him? King David, just now; but all of them have told us the same thing. The battle is the Lords! It is not by might, nor by power, but by *His Spirit* that we are victorious!"

Bradey looked intently at each of their faces just as Sheng Li burst into the atrium. Not wanting to miss out, he had decided to follow them, although he knew he could not run as fast as they. He had mounted his steed and charged down the mountain and across the realm to Yashobam's Camp. Now, as he took in the scene before him wondering what it was all about, a rush of heavenly adrenaline made him appear winded.

Uzi and Iniko blinked at each other in amazement and then questioned in unison, "Did you *run*?"

Li grinned mischievously and said, "Fine horse; I ride." Bradey joined their laughter as Li looked at him and added, "What is happening?"

Bradey looked upwards again, squinting at the glass sphere 50 feet up and said, "Where does my strength come from? My strength comes from the Lord, the Maker of Heaven and Earth. The Spirit of the Lord is upon me, to fight, and to win!"

THE LITTLEST WARRIOR

With those last words he sprang upwards, catching hold of one of the thick ropes with a firm grip, and began to climb arm over arm with powerful strokes and without hesitation. When he reached the top, a shout of triumph went up from the youths below.

"Come on!" Bradey called over his shoulder. "We have learned the secret of the warrior's strength!"

Following Bradey's example, they all made the same confession. "Where does my strength come from? My strength comes from the Lord…The Spirit of the Lord is upon me…" and they swung into action with exuberant vigor, muscles rippling until they reached the top.

Swinging to the sides and hoisting themselves through the openings to the auditorium above, they were surprised by an eruption of boisterous laughter that filled the room. Clambering to their feet, they craned their necks toward the platform where they saw Grant Finlay's massive frame resting against a wall. They rushed toward him, all talking at once.

"We did it! We learned the secret! It was amazing!"

"I know!" He chuckled. "That's why I'm here."

"What do you mean?" Uzi queried.

"Your mentors have monitored your training carefully; the King has had his eye on you. He knew this would be the day that the secret of the warrior's strength would be revealed in your spirits. He waits for you now with Yashobam at His banquet hall. You will dine with Him tonight, for He has good news for you. Go quickly, and prepare yourselves for an audience with His Royal Highness, Our Lord Jesus Christ."

Bradey and his friends were off like gazelles to their quarters to change out of their work duds and into proper attire for dining with the King. They were so excited as they talked to each other and wondered why they were being singled out; but there was a surprise in store for them. For when they arrived at the Royal Banquet Hall they saw that there were quite a few young men from other squads that they recognized from their training exercises.

Bradey scanned the group; there were ten or twelve of them. He saw Reece Ryder across the room and gestured enthusiastically as if to poke him in the chest, meaning, "You're the man!" a common accolade among fellow recruits on the field. Ryder nodded, returning Bradey's wide grin. He didn't know what the Lord was about to do, but he was more curious by the minute. Especially because he had noticed every one of these particular recruits at different times throughout their time at Camp Conquest; and all of them had impressed him with their skills, strength or character. Whatever they were getting together for, he felt very satisfied that he was included in the same group as these young warriors.

Yashobam was present, and soon called the group to order asking the boys to find their seats. There were name cards at each place setting and as he searched for his own, Bradey wondered about the seating arrangement. By the expressions on the others' faces, he could tell that they were curious as well. They shuffled about finding their spots and soon stood attentively behind their chairs awaiting the entrance of King Jesus into the hall. A herald with a trumpet

THE LITTLEST WARRIOR

announced his arrival with a musical peal of perfect notes and the Light of the Lamb filled the room. All eyes on The Master, young hearts beat proudly with the honor of their commission as He took his place at the head of the banquet table.

"Thank you for being so prompt!" He grinned, scanning the eager faces before Him. "I have waited eagerly for this day and I have much to tell you. But first, we will eat! Please sit, and enjoy the feast that has been prepared for us."

As always, trays of steaming food and pitchers of refreshing drinks were served swiftly and with skillful bearing. The servers scurried about with elegant poise and seemed to know what each young man wanted before he had a chance to ask. Bradey especially enjoyed multiple servings of hot, crusty bread with soft, melty butter; and when a divinely inspired chocolate cheesecake was served, he slowly savored the first bite and wondered whether his earthly family had ever tasted anything so fine.

The room was filled with laughter and animated conversation; but the happy sounds of feasting and fellowship faded briefly as Bradey's thoughts deepened. He suddenly thought of Anchorr and wondered who on the earth was now in his charge. So many soldiers had died since the day Christ, the Commander in Chief, had dispatched a myriad of warring angels to the battles below. Bradey and his friends had often been privileged to escort a soldier—sometimes whole groups of them at once—who had fallen in the wars of earthly kingdoms and had been transported through the Golden Gate to meet their Maker. Bradey considered it an honor to meet these brave men who had given their lives for the safety of others, and it was often his own Guardian, Anchorr, who ushered them in.

I have had more adventures than any boy could imagine; and eternity is still ahead of me; he thought pensively. *I have seen the history of the world and studied the greatest battle strategies at The Chronicles of Time and Eternity; I have worshipped the Lamb of God from the Pinnacle of Praise and heard my own voice echo from the cliffs of Mount Imminent; I have sat with my warrior brothers around the bonfires of The Presence and heard firsthand accounts of God's miraculous intervention in the affairs of men by the greatest warriors, priests and kings of all time. What an honor to be here among these giants of the faith; and to be chosen for the ranks of The Almighty.*

Suddenly he felt humbled by this great privilege and glanced to the head of table with deep-felt reverence. Jesus was looking straight into his eyes, and he smiled knowingly and nodded his acknowledgement to his "Littlest Warrior", who was not so little anymore. Bradey felt small and powerful all at the same time beneath the gaze of the Lord of All, and smiled back at him as he began to speak. If there could be such a thing as a gentle yet booming voice, it was His—the Lion and the Lamb. It filled the banquet hall, commanding attention and calming the soul all at once. He loved his boys; and they loved Him back.

"I have called you here," the Lord began as their fine feast came to a close, "because you have come to the end of your general training Camp Conquest. All of you have been highly commended by your mentors and instructors as excellent young warriors. You are ready to move to the next level of preparation where you will train as a group under Yashobam himself. You are to be a battalion; and Bradey Josheb Markis is to be your leader."

His smile broadened as astonishment flooded Bradey's youthful countenance.

"Bradey, please come forward to accept your new trust."

Bradey came forward amid shouts and cheers from his fellows, and knelt before the towering frame of his Lord and King. Drawing a large, shining sword from a decorative scabbard held by Yashobam, Jesus touched Bradey's shoulders with the blade.

"I christen this youth, through faithful service and diligent study, as leader of this battalion. Once called as my *Littlest Warrior*, I call you again;" and lowering the sword to his side, The King covered Bradey's head of wavy blonde hair with one massive palm and pressed gently as He continued. "But today, I call Bradey Josheb Markis, the man. Arise, my Warrior among Warriors."

Bradey stood, still bowing his head. If human words were to attempt a description of what he felt at this moment, it would have to be a supernatural swell of great honor, exuberant praise, deep respect and vivid anticipation enveloping him all at once. The Master placed a cloak of black velvet around his shoulders. It was trimmed in glistening white, with a bright white shield of rich silken brocade on the back. The white shield was embroidered with a curious crest in metallic threads of silver, copper, and gold.

As Bradey raised his eyes to meet his Lord's, his gaze was captivated by the bright sword that Jesus held in front of him.

"This is yours," He said simply. "But I must ask your rose in exchange."

Bradey hesitated, reaching slowly for his mother's token; the cherished gift that he had carried through all his heavenly adventures since his arrival as a rosy cherub riding on Anchorr's shoulders. He slipped it from its protective sheath, fingering it with tenderness and touching each crystal tear on the stem. His eyes met the Master's as he laid his treasure in the great scarred hands and took the new sword in exchange. The twinkle in the Lion's eyes made him pause with expectation. He watched as The King placed the orange rose on the hilt of the sword, where it immediately melded into the metal as an engraved replica, glowing like the embers of a hot fire. Bradey's face lit up in a dimpled grin.

"Thank you," he said with evident gratitude.

Suddenly, a noisy clippety-clop echoed on the marble floor tiles of the Royal Banquet Hall. All eyes turned toward the door where a regal stallion was being brought in by Yashobam. The steed was bedecked with silver, gold, and copper threads woven into his long curly mane and tail. His coat had been brushed until it was dazzling white and on his back was a black velvet coverlet trimmed in bright, white silk. It had on it the same embroidered brocade emblem as Bradey's new cloak; and the stallion pranced as if he knew he was *the man*!

It took a double-take before Bradey recognized Cherub. He looked absolutely majestic; and larger than life in his regal attire. Bradey stood; and the dimples deepened around his mouth as he grinned widely. Yashobam came to the front and handed him the reins with a low chuckle. Then The King spoke again.

"Since you have been christened as battalion leader, I thought it was time Cherub had a promotion as well!"

"Kneel, Cherub;" Bradey responded instantly. "You have been a cherub long enough!" This quip brought ripples of laughter as Bradey stood grinning at his comrades.

Cherub lowered himself to a bowed position on one knee and Bradey tapped him lightly on each shoulder with his new shimmering sword.

"You shall no longer be called 'Cherub', for you have earned the name of a champion. From this day, therefore, I dub thee, *Hero!*"

Applause filled the room, and from the midst of the jovial warriors came an unexpected, flying, streak of fur as Whisper landed on the other side of Bradey—nearly knocking him down.

"Oh, alright!" Bradey laughed, scrubbing the big cat's head with his hand. "You shall never more be Whisper the Cub; you've earned your real name—Jangi (Jonŋ-gē′)!"

Triumphant music began to play as the hall erupted once again with cheers and shouts. Man-hugs and man-shakes were given all around as the exuberant young warriors congratulated each other; while Yashobam and

The Commander in Chief looked on with great pleasure and pride. Raj purred loudly, soaking in his fame as he prowled around the hall soliciting pats and rubs.

Bradey looked around the room. The lively activity seemed to go into slow motion as he took in every detail of this incredible occasion. If Bradey Josheb had known what a *dream* was, he would have surely believed that he was in the middle of one now. Here he was, a trained warrior of the Heavenly Realm, with a regal stallion of his own, a majestic snow leopard of the noblest line, and best of all a new band of brothers—Bradey's Battalion.

Bradey's Battalion

Shortly after the banquet with The King, Yashobam organized a Ceremony of Induction for Bradey's Battalion, which was to be the first of many; for every young warrior completing his training exercises would soon after be assigned to a battalion and christened as a Warrior of the Heavenly Realm. These activities were aligned with events on God's calendar which showed clearly that the End of Time on Earth was truly at hand.

Many earthly Soldiers of the Cross who had died as older men in human wars had joined the ranks also after a period of rest and blessing; but in this place of eternal perfection, their new bodies were as strong and young as any of Heaven's Youth who had arrived as cherubs and experienced only the perfect maturing process of the spiritual realm. Some who had entered Eternity as children long before Bradey Josheb, yet had been selected by The King to be a part of this troop, had thus come to full maturity at a time that blended perfectly with the eternal destiny of these, their brothers. The Armies of The King, therefore, featured column upon column of the most striking and powerful men imaginable from every era, and every corner of the world; and God's miraculous timing and precision was evident in them all.

They would be a sight miraculous to behold someday soon, breaking through the clouds of Earth with all the saints of the ages as Jesus Christ, Lord of Lords and King of Kings led them to victory over the evil domination that had long held the world below in its iron grasp.

THE LITTLEST WARRIOR

Before the Ceremony of Induction, Yashobam called an assembly of battalion members to the Rally Stage in the Bull's Eye of Camp Conquest. As on many other occasions, they all gathered around something like a mysterious crackling campfire. Of course, there is no night in Heaven; but nothing is impossible with God. So, for the sake of atmosphere, a shimmering veil of misty twilight hung over the camp. The "fire pit" was large, and heaped with huge sparkling diamonds which, when lit by a hot coal brought swiftly on the wings of cherubim from the Throne of God, were ignited into glowing embers that emitted gold, orange and white-hot flames, bringing The Presence right into their midst for a setting of holy reverence before Almighty God (who delighted, by the way, in watching and participating—in his diverse and phenomenal forms—in the activities of His children all over His Kingdom).

Yashobam began in his low, inspiring voice, which never failed to bring his listeners to rapt attention.

"In addition to the accolades from your superiors, there are other important elements about each of you which augment your value to this battalion. The purpose of this meeting is to acquaint you with one another: your birthplace, your heritage, your God-given attributes and your assigned purpose in The Ultimate Plan. Hence, I will call each of you to my side to introduce you—in detail—to your brothers; beginning with you, Iniko." He pointed out Bradey's beaming buddy; one which he had felt such a strong connection to at their first meeting, so many adventures ago.

If a black boy could have red cheeks, Iniko had them now. He was amiably shy, but still very comfortable with his buddies. He stood there with his short, coiled hair shining in the soft, misty ambiance and his head slightly bowed, glancing ever so often at Yashobam and then at the onlookers with that famous bright white grin. Yashobam began with a voice of admiration, his big hand resting on the shoulder of Iniko's tall and slender frame.

"Iniko Ajani Diallo. Your name means *born during troubled times*, which you were; *he who wins the struggle*, which, you have; and *BOLD*, which you most certainly are." Then turning to the unit of listening young warriors, he continued with Iniko's confirmation.

"Iniko is of African origin. His family in Nigeria was overcome by rebel militia who killed his parents because they were believers in Christ. Iniko was abducted by these evil men and forced into slavery to a fiendish leader who treated him with unspeakable cruelty. His obedient nature and his faithfulness to God angered his captors, whose torturous conduct eventually took his life. Iniko stands before us as a conqueror that has prevailed over his enemies. He brings courage and dependability to our company of warriors; and he runs like the wind!" Yashobam chuckled and offered Iniko the man-shake.

A rousing cycle of cheers, accolades and supportive camaraderie followed this first introduction; and would follow the presentation of each of the other members as well. The youths would look at their friends in a new light of honor and respect after hearing their stories; and the bond of brotherhood would thicken with each induction. Sheng Li was called next.

"Sheng Li: *Victorious and powerful*! Born in Communist China to Christian parents, Sheng Li's father courageously worked in his own print shop to produce materials for The Cause. He was arrested for this, and later tortured and imprisoned because he would not reveal the names of other believers. Sheng Li—a lad of seven years at the time—became ill while he and his mother were in hiding. He was ushered into glory and stands with us now as a shining star. He is sharp and alert, and brings his gifts of perception and good judgment to the squad."

Uzi was called; and if, in God's Heaven, there could have been tears of empathy for a child in peril, Yashobam would have shown them now. He spoke soberly, with the fear of God in his voice for haters of the Jewish people.

"Uzi Seth-Kenan Zacharee: *power and strength; appointed to take possession; God has remembered.* Uzi entered Heaven's gates from a place called Auschwitz during a historical rampage by one of the lower kingdom's most murderous dictators. Separated from his parents by this evil regime that sought to annihilate the Jewish race, Uzi Seth-Kenan spent two days and nights on a frightening train ride to the death camp with many other Jewish children. When he lifted his 5-year old voice to Jesus for help, and was asked who this Jesus was, his answer amazed even the angels of Heaven; for he gallantly proclaimed, "He is the Savior of the World; Jesus is our only hope." Because of him, 42 other children cried out to Jesus from those chambers of death; and when his cherub soul was transported to glory that day, he brought 42 other tiny souls with him into the loving arms of King Jesus. Uzi contributes a spirit of valor for his fearless heroism, even as a small earthly boy. His gift of persuasion rallied Jewish children to hope in Christ; and His God has remembered."

Yashobam called each young warrior in turn, taking the time to share their valiant stories with the brotherhood, each equally endearing to the eyes of the Heavenly Realm, and their gifts equally valuable to The Ultimate Plan.

Jabari Faris Mansour was of Arabian descent. His name meant *Fearless Knight; One Who Triumphs*. He was a bodyguard for a wealthy Moroccan salt merchant, Mustafa Hakeem, who regularly travelled the trade route from Timbuktu to Cairo during the 12th century. On one trip across the desert, Jabari was converted to Christianity by a slave who was being sold at the end of the line. When the merchant master's caravan was attacked by bandits at night, Jabari was fatally wounded while protecting him and left for dead in the middle of the Sahara Desert. He awoke to new life, and a promotion, in Christ's eternal kingdom. He was loyal and brave, which noble attributes would now benefit the battalion.

Nevan Kane, *Little Saint, in battle*, lived in 15th century Ireland. His home was in Bantry Bay where his family fished for pilchard and herring to sell for export to Spain. His drunkard father spent most of their earnings on whiskey and died at the ripe old age of 38, leaving 14-year old Nevan to support his mother and two small sisters. Hard times were relieved when Nevan came across an Anglican priest from Northern Ireland who was evangelizing the Catholic lands. Through his comfort and kindness, and help with the fishing business, the Kane family came to Christ. They eagerly spread their newfound faith all along Ireland's southwest shores as Nevan grew to manhood, eventually adding a wife and children of his own to their family home. He was able to provide a substantial

THE LITTLEST WARRIOR

livelihood for all of them before he died defending his fishing vessel from Spanish pirates in the waters of the Atlantic Ocean. He brought faithfulness and strength of hand to his band of brothers.

Scandinavian, Gunnar Jens, (*Battle Warrior; God is gracious*) and Russian Prince, Ivan Alexei (*Defender*) met according to The Ultimate Plan—unbeknown to either teen. Gunnar learned of Christianity as a boy in Iceland when his Viking grandfather, Trygg Sigourney, was converted to the faith by the friendship and testimony of an Armenian missionary named Petrus. Trygg was a tribal leader who had cast his influential vote to Christianize the island in order to prevent civil war. The *Althing*—council of Viking chieftains—was swayed by his influence in their hurry to prevent violence in Icelander settlements. The rough and powerful Norse warriors—steeped in their mythological legends—were regularly threatening the newly converted patches of Christian settlers for abandoning their pagan heritage. Angered by Sigourney's influence in the council, new threats to his family moved him to send his grandson to Russia to escape the violence. Gunnar was only 15 when he set out with a seafaring crew on his grandfather's long ship, The Bjorn, across the Baltic Sea with a message to Rurik, Duke of Kiev. Rurik and Sigourney had been Viking raiders together in their young and foolish days and had remained good friends. He heartily welcomed Gunnar—the grandson of his lifelong friend—who became like a brother to Rurik's son, Ivan. Gunnar so enthusiastically shared his faith with his new friend, that Prince Ivan became a fervent Christian which caused his pagan father to send them both to the front lines of battle. Exemplary warriors, Ivan Alexei and Gunnar Jens died back to back in the Byzantine wars, and entered Heaven's Gates as brothers for Eternity, bringing fervent dedication and masterful fighting techniques to their squad.

Leo Dante was an Italian whose name meant *Lion Everlasting*. He was the lone survivor of a family of nine who became victims of the bubonic plague—The Black Death—that ravished his home town of Naples, Italy. Determined to survive, he carved wooden crosses and figurines to sell, which drew the attention of the famous Florentine sculptor, Donato di Niccoio di Betto Bardi. Donatello adopted Leo as an understudy and took him on his travels, also leading him to Christ. He learned of the Bible hero, David, as they worked together on the famous bronze, life-sized figure of the shepherd boy with the head of Goliath at his feet. Grateful for Donatello's guardianship, Leo was a faithful—and talented—steward in Renaissance art; but he had determined that he would grow to be a great warrior some day, just like David of old, and prayed fervently for an opportunity to "fight for the Almighty". He died a wealthy Italian sculptor; but God remembered his request and ushered him straightway into Camp Conquest for training. He was ecstatic, and added abundant enthusiasm and creativity to the ranks of Heaven's elect.

"Stefan Kaiser," Yashobam continued, "*Crown Leader.* You boldly rebelled against your Nazi commanders of the Reich Security in order to help Jewish people escape their would-be captors. You warned whole families whose names were on Heydrich's list to be marked with yellow stars for deportation to Poland's ghettos and then to killing camps. Your bravery saved many lives before you were caught and punished by firing squad. Little did your evil superiors know that the bullets that took your earthly life, brought you into eternal glory; and what has not been revealed to you

THE LITTLEST WARRIOR

until now, is that your courageous Christianity in the face of certain death was instrumental in the later conversion of two fellow officers and one of your commanders, who will be united with us as brothers at the end of time. Your boldness and determination is a gift to your comrades."

Shouts and cheers went up all around as Stefan received his man-shake from Yashobam and stepped down from the platform. Damien Xander was called next.

He was a Greek whose name meant *"to tame, subdue; defender of men"*. Born in the Piraeus, Damien grew up tending his father's olive groves in the plains of the Cephisus River. He often looked toward the great city of Athens, where the buildings on the summit of the Acropolis were dwarfed by the towering statue of Minerva Promachus, with shield and spear glittering in the sun.

Xander's people were proud of their strength, telling and re-telling stories of the heroes of the legendary Athenian wars. As followers of Zeno, they were polytheistic Stoics—believing in all the gods of Greek mythology and that all of nature was divine. They lived by reason and boasted as supreme beings, in a universe where they believed all matter was Deity originating from the divine fire of Zeus—and would one day be absorbed into that fire again to start all over.

Damien was at the docks when the Apostle Paul's vessel landed at Piraeus and was instantly drawn to this rough, muscular man with eyes of deepest passion. Strapping a load of olives and oil on two mules, he hurriedly followed this curious figure through the city gate. He watched this man stroll the colonnade, curiously noting the many objects of Greek devotion:

statues of Neptune, Jupiter and Apollo, of Mercury and Hercules, on platforms and columns everywhere he turned.

Later, as Paul stood on Mars Hill in the shade of the bronze champion of Athens, he boldly declared to this pagan audience that the only truth in their religion was the altar erected TO THE UNKNOWN GOD. As Damien listened intently to this stranger denying the power of every carved Deity displayed around him, he heard that the one True God was personal; not a part of the universe, but the Creator of it. That He did not dwell in any of Athens' great temples but, as the Father of all men everywhere, called every human being to repentance through His son, Jesus Christ, whom He raised from the dead to reign forever. The preacher implored the men of Athens to seek this true God and to live for His ultimate purpose, before the great Day of Judgment that would come upon all mankind.

Damien Xander went home stricken to the core. In the city of more gods than men, his family had been led astray from the only God who could save their eternal souls. Damien put his trust in Christ that day, and joined the Christians of Athens where he learned the ways of God. As he harvested olives year after year, his only weapon was the stick he used to knock the hard fruits from the branches. He knew he would never realize his boyhood dream of fighting his way to greatness as the heroes he used to worship. But with joy he served His Savior, with no inkling that he would one day join the Forces of Heaven to conquer the master of all evil in the War of all Wars. His grateful heart and fervent devotion would now be added to Bradey's Battalion.

THE LITTLEST WARRIOR

"Come up here, Cordero!" Yashobam said with his wide grin and a beckoning gesture. "You have come to the fold, my boy, where you are forever safe." As Cordero leaped to the platform and stood before Yashobam, the great warrior put both hands on his shoulders.

"Cordero Milagro Joaquin; *little lamb, a miracle, raised by Yaweh.* Your earthly pilgrimage was brief and fraught with terror; but now you will fight back, and you are on the winning side!"

Yashobam told of Cordero's boyhood in 16th century Spain during the Inquisition, when King Philip II authorized morbid forms of torture for all Protestants who would not recant their Lutheran doctrines and return to the Catholic Church. Being devout Christians, the Joaquin family would not reject their Lord, and the children were separated and forced to hard labor in the prison. First, however, they were made to watch their parents burned alive at the stake; while the Church became one small estate richer by confiscating their land. Cordero was the youngest, and served his cruel prison guard masters from nine years old until he was sixteen. Then he contracted pneumonia and died, but not without wealth; for he had shined the Light of Christ so brightly, despite his circumstances, that 25 other prisoners had found hope in Jesus through Cordero's Christian testimony. He added perseverance and a servant's heart to the band.

Next to last was Reece Ryder, Bradey's cowboy buddy with which he had already had so many marvelous adventures. Bradey had already heard a lot about Ryder's earthly life in the wild country of the Australian bush. Reece's name meant *"running knight, mounted warrior"*. His father was a British criminal brought to Sydney Cove in the mid-1800s on a Convict Ship. He was mean as a wild bore and widely known for his violent temper. Reece's mother was raised on a Brumby ranch at the base of the Blue Mountains. She grew up breathing dust, breaking wild horses and riding bareback all over the Blue Mountain wilderness. So Reece was born to a rough, uncultured family of loud scrappers. But in 1902 when the rural tent revivals came to New South Wales, Beau Ryder stopped in one night to pick a fight and got saved instead. The next night he put his wife and three kids on horseback and rode back to the tent meeting where the power of God fell and the whole Ryder family met Jesus for the first time. Their lives were transformed and their business prospered. They spent Sundays in Sydney for morning church services and afternoons at the beach. But when Mrs. Ryder was struck by typhoid fever and died, Beau sold the ranch and moved into Sydney where their church family could comfort his children in their loss. Reece was thirteen by then, and pined for their home in the wild. His dad finally let him take a job rounding up Brumbies for the breeder who bought their ranch. One stormy night on the mountains above his old home, he took a tumble with a skittish stallion and woke up in Heaven. Now he was a regular at Champion Ranch, riding the horses of Heaven. His skill with The Master's steeds was unquestionable and he was the best rider in the squadron.

"And last, but not least," Yashobam said, extending a hand; "your captain. Bradey, please step forward."

Bradey rose from his sprawling position next to the flames of The Presence, where he always loved to look deep into the glowing gems and wonder about God, the Father. Yashobam continued in a low, solemn voice.

THE LITTLEST WARRIOR

"Bradey Josheb Markis; *broad-shouldered one; descendant of powerful men*". You have a large capacity for matters of the heart. My namesake: one who will rescue, restore and bring back his people. Bradey was called away from his earthly home as an infant, entering our Lord's Kingdom as His *Littlest Warrior*. He has grown in wisdom and stature, excelling in all that the Master has required of him. Under my supervision, he will be your Captain. Bradey has a heart of obedience; he is loyal and teachable; he brings confidence and leadership to your squadron. You can be sure that he will lead you well in all that our Commander in Chief requires of this company."

With an iron squeeze on the back of Bradey Josheb's broad neck and a strong man-shake, Yashobam nodded for him to rejoin the group; then crossed his powerful arms purposefully and continued with a meditative tone.

"There will be many opportunities throughout Eternity for you young men to function together as a unit. For, although you have been masterfully trained for the Battle of the Ages, the Ultimate Plan of our Father God will present many and varied occasions for the use of your unified skills and aptitudes. All that you have seen and learned, especially those of you who completed a pilgrimage on Earth before arriving here, is merely the tip of the iceberg in comparison to the vast and adventurous experiences of the eternal expanse that lies ahead of us."

Then with a long look at the newly formed brotherhood before him, he crossed his arms and finished briskly.

"You have been on a journey together; to the otherworldly past of your comrades. You have heard stories of your brothers' earthly experience that you will never forget. You have gained insights that will strengthen your bond as a troop; and you now realize the seamless perfection of The Master's plan in bringing you together. There are no secrets here; no elements obscured; no scar concealed. You know, and are known; you are brothers under one banner for eternity. Stand up! Shout as one!"

On their feet in an instant, Bradey's Battalion stood tall and strong, raising fists together in their bold declaration.

"One Cause! One Conqueror! One King!" over and over again.

Suddenly, Yashobam drew his sword and brandished it high overhead. "Kneel!" he shouted with a roar that seemed to explode through Heaven's atmosphere and echo sharply from hill to hill. As the warriors knelt in a group before him with Bradey at the head, Yashobam stretched his gleaming weapon over their heads and lifted his thunderous voice once more.

"I christen this troop, one and all, to the eternal service of the King of Kings; Warriors of the Heavenly Realm, Bradey's Battalion! Arise and salute!"

The sky above the camp erupted once again with praise, as the angels and saints all over the realm blended their voices in adoration to The King. The newly commissioned band of warriors stood at attention, their glowing skin prickly with the fervor of this electrifying moment. Their spirits swelled with honor to serve The

THE LITTLEST WARRIOR

Lord of Hosts, The Lamb of God, The Lion of Judah in all His glory!

"There is no Ceremony of Induction without feasting!" bellowed Yashobam then, with his famous smile. "To the Banquet Hall, all of you! We will celebrate!"

Bradey moved forward to embrace his leader and Yashobam hugged him, thumping his back with a huge fist.

"Congratulations, Captain Markis!" Then he held him by the shoulders at arm's length and added with a nod.

"The Master is waiting for us. You and I have an appointment! Our feasting will have to wait."

Yashobam and Bradey left Camp Conquest on horseback. They rode for some time at a swift pace, finally reining in before a grand palace that Bradey had only seen from a distance. It was situated not far from the base of Mount Imminent, and the rolling thunder of the mountain's mysterious, clouded peak vibrated in Bradey's chest. His breathing was hard and fast, as was Hero's; one from galloping hard and the other from the rush of a true warrior's ride.

Bradey bound from his prancing steed and thought it seemed, for some reason, a farther distance to the ground than he remembered. Glancing back, he turned to give his horse's broad neck a series of hard, appreciative pats. Then stroking his beautiful mane, he noticed that it was beginning to look more and more like his sires: long locks of white gold reaching nearly to his knees.

"Hey, boy;" Bradey whispered, curving his gloved palm over the bridge of the stallion's tender nose. "You're all grown up now. How do you like your new name?"

Hero tossed his stately head and whinnied softly, prancing sideways as he looked down at his master; a far cry from the rosy-cheeked babe that first took a ride on his back at The Corrals.

"Stand by, Son of The Champion. I'll be back soon!" Bradey promised with his dimpled smile; then jogged up the steps to catch Yashobam who waited at the door of the King's mansion.

THE LITTLEST WARRIOR

"I have never seen this place!" Bradey marveled, taking in the grand architecture of marbled gold. "Where are we, sir?"

Yashobam grinned widely, showing the split between his teeth.

"This is one of many mansions that The King frequents in His Heaven. It is a place of counsel, where future events are conveyed and discussed; at least, that has been my experience here. We shall see."

He grasped a thick silk cord and pulled firmly, his arm rippling. A peal of musical bell-tones resonated deeply as the great doors opened before them. Ministering angels met them at the threshold and ushered them through the inner courtyard where petite but splendorous pear trees, cherry trees and pomegranate bushes surrounded three staggered fountains. Bluebirds and bright parakeets twittered and trilled, and the sweet perfume of something like Jasmine hung in the air.

Entering a velvet-draped room, where crystal vases held exquisite arrangements of giant white lilies and rich-textured irises, they walked across a wide white marble floor with long-stemmed red roses literally embedded into the gleaming stone. Harpists on window seats before tall gold-paned windows played softly, filling the room with peace and pleasant melody. The heavenly guides turned gently then and held up a hand to stop them about ten feet from the next entrance. It was not a door, but a diamond, faceted perfectly to fill the doorway. It had no hinges, nor handles, but spun slowly in place, reflecting the Light of the Lamb from within the next room and acting as a prism to send rainbows of light in all directions. Then the massive gem spun slightly to one side, allowing passage to Him who is more precious than diamonds, the Rose of Sharon and Lord of All.

The warriors fell to one knee, with arms crossed over their hearts, bowing in reverence to their Commander in Chief. Bradey had never seen his Lord this way before, and his heart pounded with awe. He was dressed in battle gear from head to foot. His hair was glistening white under a jeweled helmet of gold, and his eyes were fiery red. He held a spear that no man could carry and his voice was deep, yet gentle as he looked down upon them.

"We go to Mount Imminent."

Then he touched Bradey's bowed head, sending electric anticipation up and down his spine.

"Arise, young captain; I will show you what you must do."

Outside, they mounted their steeds and set off in a gallop toward the mountain. Bradey never tired of seeing The King on Champion. What awesome strength erupted from this great stallion and his magnificent rider! Heads into the wind, manes flowing, hooves pounding the kingdom turf, the horses left the ground and flew to the heights of Mount Imminent.

Yashobam's boisterous laughter rollicked through the air when Bradey nearly toppled off Hero's backside! This was the first time his horse's hooves had ever left the ground and it took him by complete surprise! Bradey didn't even know he could do it! Then he remembered his first exhilarating ride with the King when, as a chubby cherub himself, he was lifted to

THE LITTLEST WARRIOR

Champion's back for the ride of his life. He would never forget flying through the air like that: the grace, the power, the freedom! Now his thick, sunny locks flowed out behind him like Hero's mane as he guided his own champion through the skies of heaven's realm; and he shouted with boyish excitement.

"AWESOME!" Then thrusting a gloved fist into the air he yelled again, his voice breaking into the squeaky tones of teen enthusiasm, "Yes! This is _totally_ awesome!"

Leaning precariously to one side to look at the stallion's feet, he was astonished to see that they were galloping just as though they were on solid ground!

"Hero, look at you! You're the best!" And he slapped him soundly on the left front quarter before sitting upright on his back again. Then, thrusting both arms into the air, Bradey soared through the skies hands free like an eagle in flight; and he let out another whoop that was most likely heard all the way to Camp Conquest!

"Wooohooo!" And his youthful chuckle bounced from cloud to cloud in unison with Yashobam's raspy guffaws.

Seeing then that The King had not been distracted by the frolic but pressed intently forward to the top of Mount Imminent, Bradey sobered quickly, realizing that whatever waited for them on the mountain was very important to The Master. Soon hooves touched down at the summit and thunder rolled overhead. Lightening flashed in the clouds as the warriors and their leader dismounted and came together. Jesus removed his helmet and laid down his gigantic spear. His eyes were gentle now, deep pools of intense love, as he looked at his men and wrapped his great arms over their shoulders.

"Let us look into the near future, and see the events that are happening on the Earth."

With that he turned and commanded the heavens to open; and the portal on Mount Imminent revealed war on Earth. People were frightened; some hiding, some running. Disease was rampant in some countries; others were torn by severe natural disasters, or economic ruin. Here and there across the globe, groups of believers were gathered to hear God's Word. Sounds of singing were heard as their praises rose to the heavens and many were fervent in prayer saying, "Lord Jesus, come quickly!"

Bradey saw deep grief in his Lord's countenance, and he crinkled his brow and asked, "Lord, what must we do?"

The Lamb of God lifted his arms upward and cried out with great anguish in a loud voice.

"How long, my Father? How long will you wait to avenge my people and save them from our enemies?"

Then a great voice, that seemed to come from everywhere all at once, filled the heavens like rolls of deep thunder.

"The time has come, my Son. The cup of the Earth's iniquity is full; the reapers of the Evil One stand poised with their sickles, ready to gather the souls of men. Those who have believed in you await your prophesied return. As it is written, so let it be done!"

THE LITTLEST WARRIOR

A lightening storm like nothing Bradey had ever seen erupted on top of Mount Imminent; but, of course, there is no fear in Heaven so it was a breathtaking display; and positively mesmerizing to the two warriors. In the midst of it, however, with a voice like His Father's, Jesus looked through the portal and cried out like the sound of many waters.

"I have come that they may have LIFE! And have it to the full!"

Then he turned around, and His glorious countenance shone like the sun. The two warriors hid their faces as their Lord and King shouted across His Heaven.

"Prepare the way of the Lord! Prepare the Marriage Supper of the Lamb; for The King will soon return with His Bride!"

Then he was on the back of The Champion and they were off like a flash, leaping into the deep, cool mist of the mountainous ravine below.

"Come!" Yashobam beckoned. And the two of them mounted their steeds and leaped into the blue mist after their Lord.

The ride down was every bit as exciting as the ride to the top of the mountain, but Bradey's mind was consumed with the excitement of the moment. Christ was returning to Earth! But before the Final Battle—in which the Armies of Heaven were even now preparing to engage—He would rescue His Bride from the wrath of God that would soon fall upon a world that had rejected Him. Every eye would see Him in the clouds, but The Bride of Christ—His faithful followers worldwide—would actually join Him in the air to be escorted into the heavenly kingdom! Bradey's own earthly family would surely be among them, for he was certain that they shared his zeal for The Ultimate Plan of the Ages; and that each one had found the same devotion to Christ on their earthly pilgrimage as he had found in Heaven. His mind was reeling with emotion as Hero's hooves clopped onto the Golden Road and slowed to an easy trot.

The Heavenly Realm, however, was in high gear! Everywhere he turned, Bradey saw people and angels hurrying from place to place in response to the King's command. They were preparing for the arrival of the Bride of Christ; making the final preparations for the Marriage Supper of the Lamb! Singing and laughter filled the air. As happy a place as Heaven was, the joy in the atmosphere had *never* reached the level that was now attained. Something great and amazing was on the horizon.

As the horses pranced to a stop in front of the palace, Bradey saw Champion quietly grazing in the side pasture and realized that The Master had arrived way ahead of them. Ministering angels once again met them at the gate of the outer court and ushered them through the Room of Harps.

This time they were led down a bright, wide hallway to a long side room with a golden altar at one end. Behind the altar, The King sat on a brilliant throne bedecked with rubies and sapphires. He was dressed in a robe of gleaming white now, and wore a golden crown. His eyes were glistening with anticipation, and He smiled as Yashobam and Bradey approached. They knelt before the altar, crossing their arms over their hearts, and then rose to stand before Him. Yashobam stepped back respectfully then, knowing that The King would speak only to Bradey. Jesus descended from the throne and moved to the altar, lifting the top as a lid and retrieving several garments. Closing it again, He laid them neatly on top of the altar and spoke softly.

"Bradey Josheb, you are expecting company!" His smile broadened as he added, "and when they arrive, you will need these."

He held out one of the garments which Bradey took from his hands. He recognized it instantly. It was a cloak of black velvet, trimmed in glistening white, with a bright white shield of rich silken brocade on the back, just like his—the one The Lord had placed over his shoulders at his christening. Bradey turned it over to examine the curious crest embroidered in metallic threads on the white shield—as he had done so many times before to his own cloak. Now he had to know.

"What is this, my Lord?" He looked up with wondering eyes. "I must know, for I feel a bond to this symbol that I do not understand."

The King chuckled knowingly, "I'm sure you do, for it is the Markis Crest; and these," he added, laying two more identical cloaks in his arms, "are for your brothers. The silver threads are for Pure Devotion, the copper for Eternal Truth, and the gold for The Royal Crown—my authority under which you will all serve together for Eternity. As for the symbols, you must wait for your father to clarify these; for the crest is his design."

He paused here and chuckled again as Bradey's face lit up like a light. Then with a gentle squeeze on His young warrior's shoulder, He added, "and I am very certain that he would love nothing more than to explain it to his fourth son."

The Master of Heaven's Realm straightened now and looked upward, his expression of gentle grace swallowed by a sudden look of intensity. With a passionate tone, he walked around the altar and headed toward the door.

"I must go." Stalking resolutely across the long floor, he turned his head slightly and called to Bradey over his shoulder as He left the room.

"I will return soon; meet us at Heaven's Gates;" and He was gone.

Before a word could be spoken between them, the voice of the archangel encompassed the Realm like a sonic boom and the Trumpet of God shook Heaven and Earth. The warriors vanished into thin air and Bradey felt himself being propelled through a distantly familiar vacuum of light and strength; a vibrant, moving radiance, speeding toward the earth.

In the next instant, he penetrated six feet of earthly soil and his soul re-entered a tiny human frame.

The ground opened immediately and in another millisecond his infant body sped upwards, into his mother's arms; as she and all his earthly family ascended swiftly toward a bright light where The King of Kings waited in the clouds.

The *next* instant, he stood again on the inside of Heaven's Gates: fully grown, well clad, and wrapping the crested cloaks over the shoulders of his brothers three as they entered the Eternal Realm.

THE LITTLEST WARRIOR

They were all surprised; so much had happened all at once! A man's voice interrupted their reunion.

"Bradey Josheb!" He turned to see his father standing with arms crossed and a broad smile. "You're wearing the crest! Looks good, son!"

The brothers, suddenly realizing who they were looking at erupted in varied responses. One said,

"No way! What's up, bro?" Another exclaimed,

"Dude! Look at the hair!" And the third,

"Hey, Bradey! Do I get a sword like that?"

Then he heard it—the sweetest voice that ever landed on a boy's ears.

"Bradey? Is that you?"

His eyes darted about and, spotting her a few feet away on his left, he turned sideways with his dimpled grin and looked his mother full in the face, holding out both hands.

"Hi, Mom. Welcome to The Master's Heaven."

Then placing a tiara of diamonds and orange rosebuds on her head, he kissed her on the cheek. He could tell by the look on her face that she was in great wonderment over who her little boy had become; but she'd get used to it. He just winked and pulled a package from his vest.

"I have something for the Little Rainbow," he said, squatting down to hand it to his cherubic sister.

It was the treasure box of pearl and gold that he had gotten from Robert at Lake Aquarium so many adventures ago, not knowing why. As he placed it in her tiny hands, she squealed with delight. Then she reached for him, and he perched the Little Rainbow high on his shoulders. Looking back at his mother—who was still in awe of him—he smiled broadly again and bent slightly forward, touching the silvery Mother's Kiss on his wide, bronze forehead.

"See there?" He said with arching eyebrows, and blonde curls falling around his handsome face. "There's your mark."

There was a long pause, as a crystal tear of joy slipped down her angelic cheek.

"Okay, then!" She smiled brightly; and slipped her slender, petite hand into his big strong one.

"How about a first class tour?"

Made in the USA
San Bernardino, CA
15 January 2014